The Silent Auction

Other Books by this Author

The Bronxville Book Club

The Silent Auction

Pamela Hackett Hobson

iUniverse, Inc.
New York Lincoln Shanghai

The Silent Auction

iUniverse, Inc.

For information address:
iUniverse, Inc.
2021 Pine Lake Road, Suite 100
Lincoln, NE 68512
www.iuniverse.com

The Silent Auction is a work of fiction. Names, characters, places and incidents either are the product of the author's imagination or are used fictitiously.

ISBN: 0-595-31377-9 (Pbk)
ISBN: 0-595-66304-4 (Cloth)

Printed in the United States of America

For my silent partners,

Bob, Tom and Mike

~

Acknowledgments

Bob, Tom and Michael have blessed my life in ways I never could have imagined. Patty and Peggy, to borrow from a great song, "there never were such devoted sisters." Dad, Barbara, Joe, Greg, and all my nieces and nephews, thank you for your unwavering support, love and continued belief in me. Allison, you could write a book on being a good friend. Each of these individuals has my eternal gratitude.

To Elizabeth, Karen, Madeleine, Debbie, Cynthia, Anne, and Ann and all my other friends and book club members who contributed to my success and unselfishly rejoiced for me, thank you. Leslie, your thoughtful birthday card was inspirational.

And last but not least, thanks to my "nine-to-five" family—Carole, Violeta, Yvonne, Chandra, Roe, Maureen, Tony, 3X, Mike, Millie, Terry— and the rest of the gang at 10 Exchange.

The Silent Auction

"Live in such a way that you would not be ashamed to sell your parrot to the town gossip."

Will Rogers

Table of Contents

Prologue

Majestic Manor

This Masterton Woods estate in the charming village of Bronxville invites you to recapture the age of elegance.

Ascend the sweeping driveway of this stone mansion with graceful Tudor gables and leaded, stained glass windows, to enter your new home. Warm yourself by the substantial fireplace in the reception room while pausing to admire the classic Bowman architectural touches.

You'll entertain in style in the generously proportioned rooms with 12-foot high ceilings throughout the first floor. Recently renovated gourmet kitchen and solarium retain the old-world charm while ensuring every modern comfort. A grand 3-story staircase takes you to the Master suite and marble bath, and 6 additional bedrooms for family members and guests.

Surrounded by sweeping lawns, an expansive stone terrace overlooks the in-ground pool. Exceptionally private setting.

To apply for an appointment to view this village treasure, please contact
Kathryn Chasen
Certified Real Estate Professional
www.hlre.net

"People who work sitting down get paid more than people who work standing up."

Ogden Nash

Chapter 1

The Braithwaites of Bronxville

I've Been Moved.

Morgan Braithwaite IV didn't work for IBM—or **I've Been Moved**, as his father always referred to the elite company that recruited him from Harvard's Class of '58. Morgan's career aspirations, and the resulting international postings, were tied to Global OmniMedia, a highly respected entertainment company with a mission to dominate the competition in each of its core businesses. His colleagues had their own nickname for their "parent" company—Good Old Mom—or GOM, for short.

Prior to moving over to GOM's Phresh Division, an acknowledged leader in the urban record label and music publishing field, Morgan had held a number of senior executive positions in GOM's other businesses. For the last five years, he had headed up the broadcasting and book publishing ventures as part of the company's succession plan mandated by their Board of Directors. During his steady rise to the top tier on the organization chart, he had been exposed to operations all over the world, with two-year assignments in San Francisco, Washington, Luxembourg, Tokyo, Australia, London…and now New York.

The six-foot-two, sandy-haired executive, his petite, dark-haired wife, Brooke, and their three growing children had endured more than their fair share of relocations as Morgan ascended each rung on the steep corporate ladder. With the children getting older, Brooke was hopeful that the family would be able to put down roots in New York. Bronxville, New York, to be exact. From all that she had heard, Bronxville appeared to be the ideal location for the Braithwaite family.

Of course, GOM provided everything the family would need for a stress-free move. Its Corporate Relocation Division had selected *Houlihan Lawrence*, a highly respected real estate firm, to assist Brooke in finding the perfect house in Bronxville to suit the family's needs. Kathryn Chasen, the dedicated real estate agent assigned to the family, had been the consummate professional throughout the entire process. Kathryn had lived in the village for many years and had worked for one of *Houlihan Lawrence's* fiercest competitors before joining their team. She knew a tremendous amount about all the houses, the school, the local country clubs, shopping, and other amenities available to village residents.

At their first meeting, Kathryn had shared with Morgan and Brooke that Bronxville was often called the village "that is endlessly copied but never matched." Located in southern Westchester County, Bronxville had a well-earned reputation as a charming English-style village only 18 miles from Manhattan. Both Brooke and Morgan felt they would have the best of both worlds—all the nearby cultural opportunities that New York City had to offer, while still being able to live in a small affluent village where children still walked to school and neighbors got to know one another.

Kathryn educated the Braithwaites on the unique history of the village. As an 1895 sales brochure by Alice Wellington Rollins promised, "...we are ourselves a society. We all know each other, and you cannot come to our Park anyway unless some of us know and like you. You must be either a Genius or a Delightful Person to be eligible at all for such privileges as we extend." Brooke and Morgan had laughed at Ms. Rollins' sentiment. Certainly no one in their family was a genius, but perhaps some of the current residents in the village would find one or all of them to be delightful.

Speaking of delightful, the three Braithwaite children were the prime reason the family decided to relocate from London to Bronxville instead of accepting yet another overseas posting. Brooke's career was her family, and she was growing increasingly frustrated that every time she succeeded in getting the children established in a school, with new circles of friends for all of them, it was time to pack up. She had been quite clear with Morgan that she hoped this move to Bronxville, New York, would be their last for the foreseeable future. As the son of an expat, Morgan didn't need Brooke to convince him that their living situation needed to be more stable. He had assured her that GOM would keep him in New York at least until Spencer left for college.

Spencer, a tall, gangly teenager, who was about to enter high school, needed more stability as he began the increasingly important academic years leading up to the high-stakes college admissions game. The fair-haired middle child, Charlotte, was ten years old and ready for fifth grade. Their "baby," Jayne, would be celebrating her 7th birthday this summer and entering the second grade in the fall. Given the different ages of the children, the Braithwaites needed a top notch school that would meet the diverse needs of their family.

The Bronxville School most definitely had an excellent reputation. Their new neighbor Lizbet Wellington Smith (surely not a descendant of that Wellington Rollins woman who had written the original sales brochure!) had shown Brooke the results of a study by *Worth Magazine* that noted that those who attended Bronxville High School had better odds of getting into an Ivy League school. Bronxville—in the esteemed company of such schools as Spence, Phillips Exeter Academy, and Hackley—was one of only six public high schools that made it into the top 100 on this prestigious list. The school was wonderful, but Lizbet had cautioned Brooke that she must *immediately* arrange for private tutors for *all* of her children, even Jayne, since it was never too early to start preparing for the college admissions game. According to

Lizbet, at least 75% of the high school students in the school had private tutoring. Lizbet offered to share the names of several wonderful tutors she had hired for her own daughter, Whitney, who was practically guaranteed early acceptance to Yale.

Certainly, Brooke and Morgan thought their children's education was very important, but they wanted to look beyond the average SAT and Advanced Placement scores, and beyond the number of graduates who were accepted at Princeton, Georgetown and Yale (and even the number who declined Harvard!). They knew that children in public schools in wealthy neighborhoods tended to perform better on standardized tests. Perhaps it was due to the small class sizes and excellent teaching staff; or perhaps it was because the parents were more likely to be college graduates with the means to expose their children to a wide variety of extracurricular educational opportunities and individualized tutoring. Whatever the reason the students were so incredibly successful, Morgan and Brooke knew that their children would be well served in the Bronxville School. Morgan also took some comfort in his children's status as legacy applicants. He, his father and his grandfather had all graduated from Harvard and made significant monetary contributions to ensure that the family tradition continued in perpetuity.

Since Brooke and Morgan were sold on Bronxville's proximity to Manhattan and the reputation of its school, they focused on the houses, which were nothing short of incredible. As Kathryn had explained, the prominent architects whose homes graced the village included William Bates, Lewis Bowman, Penrose Stout and George Root. The particular home the Braithwaites had fallen in love with had been designed by Lewis Bowman. The typical Bowman hallmarks, such as a step-down living room, carved and decorated beamed ceilings, balcony foyer, oak-paneled library, and baronial-sized fireplaces, sealed the deal for Morgan. Brooke was sold once she entered the secluded Master Suite with an over-sized dressing room/spa bath and two generous walk-in closets. Her closet had a faux wall in the back that camouflaged the built-in jewelry safe with tarnish-resistant liners, while Morgan's closet had a specially-made tie rack that could hold over 500 of his favorite Hermès and Zegna ties.

Over the past few months as they worked through all the details of the sale, Brooke and Kathryn had developed a friendship that hopefully would continue now that the closing was behind them and Kathryn's professional services were no longer required. Physically opposite—Kathryn was tall and blonde, while Brooke was a brunette who would have difficulty meeting the height requirement for some of the rides at Rye Playland—their personalities were very much in sync.

Brooke had learned quite a bit about Kathryn as they drove around in her ice-blue Mercedes convertible. It was amazing how much they had in common, in addition to marrying prep school graduates with numerals after their last names! Divorced from P. David Chasen III, Kathryn was the mother of one child, Pryce, who was about to enter 5th grade, the same grade as Brooke's daughter Charlotte. Kathryn had a wicked sense of humor and didn't take herself too seriously. She had regaled Brooke with many hilarious anecdotes about Carlo, Pryce's handsome "Manny." Many a neighbor had assumed that the Manny was really for Kathryn, not Pryce. While Kathryn pretended to be flattered that anyone would think that she was even capable of that kind of relationship, she did actually have a brief fling with Carlo that marked her re-entry into the dating scene. Twenty years her junior, Carlo's youth and incredible looks proved to be both the best and the worst thing about him. The Concordia College girls she hired to baby-sit for Pryce while they went out actually had more in common with Carlo than she did. They flirted outrageously with him as they spoke in what seemed like another language. They at least knew, and more importantly cared, who some guy named 50 Cent was, and what those adorable newlyweds Nick Lachey and Jessica Simpson were up to on MTV. For his part, even Kathryn's Barbie dolls were older than Carlo, and he hadn't even been born when the Beatles debuted on the Ed Sullivan Show on CBS. Carlo had no idea who Topo Gigio was, but he thought Triumph the Insult Comic Dog was nothing short of brilliant.

Alas, Carlo had moved on, but then again, so had Kathryn. Recently she had begun dating Trip Thayer, an old boyfriend from college whose divorce had just become final. Trip was a tall, aging jock who lived in one of the Pondfield Road townhouses. He and his ex-wife, Claire, shared custody of their son, Jake, who was in the same grade as Kathryn's son, Pryce. David didn't seem particularly happy about his ex-wife's dating habits, but then he was no one to talk. Since he had moved back into town to be closer to Pryce, David had been seen squiring a number of good-looking women to all the local haunts. Kathryn's friends were only too happy to keep her posted on David's latest arm candy.

A wealth of information, Kathryn suggested that if Brooke wanted to meet more of her neighbors, she should get involved as a class mother at the school; join the Bronxville chapter of the Junior League; take up paddle tennis; and find a fun activity such as a book club. Kathryn and Brooke's new neighbor, Lizbet, belonged to a book club made up of a group of local women Brooke should get to know. Kathryn offered to introduce her to the others at the next meeting which would be held at her house. When Brooke told Kathryn that she thought the book club sounded like a terrific idea since she was such an avid reader, Kathryn laughed out loud. "Oh, Brooke, we don't actually read the books!"

Kathryn also gave Brooke invaluable background on all of their neighbors on Elm Rock and the surrounding cul de sacs. The people in the huge stone house on their right, Lizbet Wellington Smith and her husband Grant, had been very welcoming to the Braithwaites. At a cocktail party Lizbet had hosted in their honor, Brooke had learned that both Lizbet and Grant were both Yale graduates and had high hopes that their daughter Whitney, a senior at the Bronxville School, would follow in their footsteps. Whitney seemed like a lovely young woman, but Brooke sensed that Whitney did not share the same burning desire to go to Yale that her Mom clearly had for her. Lizbet, a petite, exquisitely dressed, ash-blonde bundle of energy, personified the über-volunteer that Brooke had encountered when she lived in similar upscale neighborhoods in Washington and

London. Brooke sensed that she had better be careful or she could end up getting involved in an overwhelming number of committees and commitments that she might not necessarily choose for herself.

Lizbet too had offered her suggestions for ways that Brooke and Morgan could get more involved in the community. The Braithwaite family had settled into their new home just in time to participate in all the Memorial Day activities that Lizbet had organized at the Bronxville School. As the main fundraiser for the PTA, the Memorial Day weekend included events and activities for all residents of the village and surrounding towns. Lizbet had given the Braithwaites a copy of the *Review Press* in which she had been interviewed about all the exciting activities that were planned. The Games Committee was bringing back old-time favorites like the Jumping Castle, Obstacle Course, and Dunk Tank that Charlotte and Jayne would love, but they were also introducing several new attractions like a rock climbing wall and skateboard ramp that Spencer could try out. Other committees were organizing a Run for Fun, Bake Sale, Art Show and gently-used book sale. Local restaurants and shops would provide food of every variety and unique boutique items for sale. As long-time *Review Press* reporter Danny Lopriore noted, all those activities traditionally were very well received, but without question, the biggest success of the weekend was always the Silent Auction.

Lizbet suggested to Morgan that he should bid on a number of the Silent Auction items as a way for the family to meet new people while contributing to a worthy cause. The Braithwaites had participated in a similar Silent Auction when they lived in Washington, and Morgan agreed that it would help ease the transition if Brooke and the kids participated in at least one event in which they would meet some of their new neighbors or classmates. With Lizbet's able assistance, Morgan put his name on several of the ribboned bidding sheets for a whole range of items. He just hoped that by the 2 P.M. closing on Monday, he would be the highest bidder on at least some of the more interesting offerings, especially the cruise for

Brooke. He loved to surprise his wife, and she could use that kind of relaxing getaway with new friends to relieve the stress of the relocation.

The weather turned out to be picture perfect for all the festivities. Brooke bought quite a few hand-made and unusual gifts at the Festival on the Green, Charlotte spent hours at the book sale, Jayne bounced herself silly in the Jumping Castle, and Spencer spent most of his time in a harness as he mastered the rock climbing wall. After spending most of the day down at the school, the Braithwaites walked the short distance to their home to enjoy their Memorial Day barbecue. While the family sat outside on the terrace with plates of filet mignon and new potatoes, their housekeeper, Mariella, approached, phone in hand. She apologized, but explained that someone named Lizbet insisted that she interrupt.

Brooke and the kids could only hear Morgan's side of the brief conversation. Although he usually became quite angry whenever the telephone interrupted the family meal, Morgan was actually smiling. Curious enough to burst, Brooke couldn't wait for him to hang up. When he did, he held up his hand to hold off questions while he asked Mariella to bring out the Silent Auction booklet from his desk in the den.

Savoring the moment, Morgan presented the booklet to Brooke and directed her attention to the items he had circled. Brooke was flabbergasted to learn that Morgan had been the highest bidder on quite a few events that would take place over the next few months. Although he told her he had been outbid on a week's stay in a Tuscany villa, and a few other exotic offerings, the ten or so items he had purchased were quite impressive and would set his bank account back several digits.

Brooke could hardly wait to get started enjoying Morgan's generosity.

"Money was never a big motivation for me, except as a way to keep score. The real excitement is playing the game."

Donald Trump

Chapter 2

Going, Going, Gone!

rooke settled into a chaise lounge on the terrace to reread the descriptions for each of the items Morgan had successfully purchased. She was really looking forward to the first event that would take place in less than three weeks.

~~~

Dinner in Style

Dinner in Style—hosted by Roger and Sarah Hamilton & Massimo and Giselle Ceravalo.

This calls for a special occasion. Roger and Sarah Hamilton will host a private dinner party for up to 12 couples at their gracious home. A gourmet meal will be prepared and served with a selection of fine wines from Roger's private wine cellar. But that's not all…After your main course, head over to Massimo and Giselle's home for some very special confections to end a perfect evening.

Menu to be determined.

Third Saturday night in June

Minimum Bid: $350 per couple.

~ ~ ~

Morgan told her that he had initially bid the $350, but Roger's wine cellar must be something because the amount quickly moved up to $500.

Brooke skipped the section on the services of personal trainers, chefs, and merry maids that were being auctioned off. After living the life of an expat for so long, those kinds of "luxuries" were commonplace for her. Morgan had always ensured that Brooke had whatever staff she needed to keep her in the manner to which she was accustomed. Even in Bronxville, with Lizbet's assistance, Brooke had already found a trainer who came to the house on Mondays and Thursdays to put her through a rigorous workout. They had interviewed a terrific Culinary Institute trained chef who had agreed to come in five times a week to cook for the family; on weekends, they usually went out for dinner or ordered take out. Of course the family's live-in housekeeper Mariella was always amenable to pitching in for special occasions. And one of Lizbet's cleaning ladies had a friend who was available Tuesdays and Fridays, but was also willing to working additional hours if Brooke was entertaining and needed an extra pair of hands.

The next section had some family events that would provide an opportunity for all of them to make some new friends. Spence probably wouldn't want to go to the pool party that Morgan had picked, but the girls would definitely love it. Even Morgan would probably enjoy the evening. With his work schedule, he didn't have enough opportunities to meet a lot of the men in the community.

~~~

Margarita Pool Party

Ladies, grab your bikini and pareo, and Gentlemen, grab your surfer shorts, and join new friends for a Margarita pool party you won't soon forget. This special evening will be hosted by Bronxville's very own gourmand, Wyatt Davenport, and his wife Samantha, in their secluded backyard oasis.

Lifeguard included.

Minimum Bid: $300 per family

Children over 5 welcome.

Maximum: Six families

~~~

Brooke scanned the list of baseball, hockey and football tickets, but it didn't appear that Morgan had tried to bid on any of the offered items. "Honey, how come you didn't go for that sports package for yourself and Spencer? Or any of those tickets to Yankees, Giants, and Rangers games?"

"Some jerk was guarding the sign-in sheet. Every time someone added his name, this guy immediately upped the bid." Morgan waved his hand dismissively. "Let him have the tickets, since that's probably the only way a guy like that will ever get seats like those. I'll just take some clients and reserve the skybox for the games Spence and I really want to see."

But as Morgan peered over Brooke's shoulder at the page she had open he did look a little disappointed.

She asked him what was wrong.

"Nothing."

Brooke wasn't buying it. She looked more closely at the sports items up for auction besides the tickets. "How about this week at the Skip Barber Racing School in Florida? You've always wanted to drive around like Bond, James Bond."

Morgan shrugged. "Maybe next time. I guess there are a lot more 007 wannabes in this town than I thought." He quickly changed the subject. "But look at the next one...I got it for our Princess Jaynie."

~ ~ ~

Happy Birthday!

Francesca Walker, your children's favorite Middle School Spanish teacher, will keep your child and ten special friends spellbound at a truly unusual birthday party. She will introduce your child to the favorite games of yore...pin the tail on the donkey; musical chairs; hot potato, and many, many more.

Minimum Bid: $500

~ ~ ~

Brooke kissed Morgan's cheek. "You're right, Jaynie will love it. I can't wait to tell her when she gets home from a play date with her friend Lily."

"I'm glad Jaynie seems to be making some friends in town. How about you? Are you getting to know any of the other mothers?"

"A little bit. Lily's mom's name is Giselle. She seems nice enough. Not that you'd be interested, but Kathryn told me that Giselle is a former model. Nowadays she keeps busy with her own business as a designer of high-end lingerie."

Morgan raised his eyebrows but knew better than to pursue that line of conversation.

Continuing through the catalogue, Brooke paused at the descriptions of unique art treasures. It wasn't surprising that Morgan skipped these items since he knew that Brooke had collected more than enough interesting objects d'art over the course of their travels.

It also wasn't surprising that he didn't bid on the redecorating consultation that sounded like it might be popular in Bronxville.

~ ~ ~

Redecorating in a day

"You've all admired Lizbet Wellington Smith's elegant home…Lizbet will share her special decorating talents to help you reinvent any room in your house. You select the room, and she will bring in a hand-picked team of professionals to rearrange the furniture, rehang artwork, and suggest color schemes, carpet choices and more.

Date and time to be mutually agreed upon.

Minimum Bid: $600

~ ~ ~

There were so many rooms in their new house, and several probably hadn't been renovated in a few years, but Morgan had confidence in Brooke's well-honed redecorating talents. With her uncanny eye for color and fabric, and the generous relocation allowance provided by GOM, the house would be a showplace in no time at all. Even if Brooke wanted another opinion, anytime Lizbet came over to their house, she was more than happy to offer unsolicited advice on their decorating challenges…and for free!

But the next item was very, very special. Brooke thought it called for a new outfit. And a new hairdo. And a French manicure…

~ ~ ~

Breakfast at Tiffany's!

Dress to the nines for an elegant day in Manhattan. Join your hostess, Madison Winthrop, for a private tour of the world famous Tiffany vaults. Following your insider's look, let's do lunch at the incomparable La Grenouille and try on selected pieces from Madison's personal heirloom collection.

Of course, car service from Bronxville to Manhattan and back again will be provided!

Minimum Bid: $750

8 Highest bidders

~ ~ ~

Brooke would most definitely enjoy this outing. Of course she had heard about Tiffany's, and received more than her fair share of robin's-egg-blue boxes as wedding presents, but somehow she had never had the opportunity to visit the famous landmark on previous excursions to New York.

Morgan was glad Brooke was looking forward to Tiffany's and hoped she wouldn't be disappointed that he hadn't been the successful bidder on a few of the other highly sought-after items. He really wanted the pair of tickets to the annual New Year's Eve gala at the Casino Ballroom on Catalina Island; that was something they had often talked about doing. He'd have to see if he could pull a few strings with some people in the Event Planning Department at GOM to buy a table.

There were a lot of golf outings, but that just didn't interest Morgan. There also was a hot-air balloon ride over the Napa Valley, complete with catered picnic and a selection of fine wines from the region. Brooke wasn't surprised Morgan didn't bid on an any kind of air adventure, no matter how unusual—he had more frequent flier miles than anyone she knew. He had circled the week's use of a condo at Kiawah Island in South Carolina, but he must have been outbid. He also had a question mark next to the two box seats for the Kentucky Derby that included hotel, airfare and a special Derby Brunch. But the derby item was only for two, and Charlotte and Jayne both loved horses. Neither would be pleased to be left behind while their father took the other.

Morgan must have chosen the next item because the whole family loved skiing, and the "cozy chalet" sounded ideal for all of them. Even if they did have to fly to Colorado, Morgan would be happy to get on a plane for a family vacation. Maybe they could even go during the Thanksgiving break when the kids were off from school and he wasn't as busy at work.

~ ~ ~

A Cozy Chalet

Spend a glorious week in a secluded retreat nestled in the Aspen Trees of West Vail. This recently refurbished home includes two master bedrooms, three additional bedrooms, five baths and a gourmet kitchen. There's an additional loft/entertainment room, and a large deck with hot tub to enjoy the breathtaking views. Located just a short distance from Vail village, Lionshead and the Cascade Club, you'll find everything you need for a spectacular getaway vacation.

No smoking, no pets, and no unaccompanied children, please.

Minimum Bid: $3,000

~ ~ ~

Brooke checked out the long list of internships by local professionals in fashion merchandising...sports management...television production. There was even an internship with a plastic surgeon. It was a good thing there wasn't a matching auction item that included the actual plastic surgery. Woe to the husband who bought that unsolicited "gift" for his wife.

The next group of items didn't include plastic surgery, but there was a whole list of grooming services for the family pet. Thankfully Morgan had skipped these items. Their Yorkie, Gilligan, didn't need a day of beauty. He was more than handsome enough.

Brooke almost missed the Landscaping Consultation that Morgan had highlighted. It was right after the Private Tour of Central Park with a local historian. Brooke was quite pleased he had thought of this. Even though they had a gardener who had come highly recommended by Kathryn, Brooke had been planning to talk to someone about the overall design of their yard. The plantings were very traditional and lovely, but Brooke knew there were opportunities to add a lot more color. She had a lot to learn about what plants and flowers worked well in this kind of climate. Besides, she had heard about Chelsea, the local landscape architect who was donating her services for the benefit of the school, and this would be a good opportunity to get to know her.

~ ~ ~

The Gracious Garden

Not sure what to put in your terrace planters, which flowers and shrubs grow best in the shade, or how to update your garden with the newest varieties of perennials? Just ask local landscape architect, Chelsea Hollingsworth. One of the premier designers of gardens for homes and estate properties, Chelsea is a member of the Association of Professional Landscape Designers and the American Horticultural Society.

Minimum Bid: $500.

~~~

The next item Morgan had selected was just for Brooke. No husband, no kids, no pets. She could hardly contain herself when she read about the cruise.

~~~

Sailing Away

Need some pampering?

Grab your best girlfriend—or better yet—all your best girlfriends and sail away on a 4 day/3 night cruise aboard the luxurious Star Princess. Each day you can choose to participate in fitness classes or select from an unbelievable array of pampering treatments—facial and nail therapies; massages and bodywork; spa hand and foot treatments; exfoliation; body wraps; hydrotherapies, and more. Enjoy gourmet meals and deluxe accommodations that will take you to a place where your everyday routines are just a memory.

Winning bidders will also receive a spa outfit designed by our very own designer, Giselle Ceravalo.

Minimum Bid: $2,000 - all inclusive

12 Highest bidders

~~~

Brooked pointed out to Morgan that the woman who was donating the spa outfit was Giselle, Lily's mother. Brooke wondered if Giselle or any of the other mothers she had met would be bidding on the cruise as well. She'd like to get to know the parents of her children's friends better.

The very last item Morgan bought was two tickets to a holiday house tour that was open to the first 150 bidders. After being in many different countries at Christmastime, Brooke would enjoy a tour of some of the most beautiful neighborhood houses all dressed up for the holidays.

~~~

Deck the halls with boughs of holly!

Usher in the season with a tour of some of the most spectacular homes in our village. The stockings will be hung from the chimney with care, chestnuts will be roasting on an open fire, and a turkey and some mistletoe will help to make the season bright.

Tour festive homes throughout the village that are all decked out for the holidays. Be sure not to miss the final stop on the tour hosted by Grant and Lizbet Wellington Smith. Sip champagne, nibble hors d'oeuvres, and sing along with the Victorian carolers as they help to make the spirit bright.

December 10
3:00–7:00 p.m.
Bid: $125 per person fixed
Maximum: 150 tickets
Tour the Homes of:
Cordelia and Oliver Wilkinson IV
Wright and Danica Corbett

Ellison and Judith Lewellyn
George and Pamela Connaught
Grant and Lizbet Wellington Smith

~ ~ ~

Brooke went to the phone to call Kathryn and tell her about Morgan's surprise. Kathryn was just coming in the door from showing a couple the turn-of-the-century Victorian that had just come on the market over on Park Avenue. Kathryn told Brooke it wasn't as charming as their house, but it was a steal at $2.95 million. She didn't think it would stay on the market very long. The property taxes were still under $30,000 a year, so that made it even more attractive.

Kathryn paused to catch her breath. "But enough about me. Did you get down to the school today for all the festivities?"

Brooke went through the litany of Silent Auction items Morgan had lined up. Kathryn was *very* impressed at Morgan's initiative, although she sensed the invisible (and beautifully manicured) hand of Lizbet behind the scenes. He had definitely made some terrific selections out of the many from which to choose, including several donated by members of the Bronxville Book Club. All things considered, Brooke would have a perfect opportunity to get to know a lot of the local residents very well over the next few months.

Maybe too well.

"At a dinner party one should eat wisely but not too well, and talk well but not too wisely."

W. Somerset Maugham

Chapter 3

Dinner in Style

~ ~ ~

Dinner in Style—hosted by Roger and Sarah Hamilton &
Giselle and Massimo Ceravalo.

This calls for a special occasion. Roger and Sarah Hamilton
will host a private dinner party for up to 12 couples at their gra-
cious home. A gourmet meal will be prepared and served with a
selection of fine wines from Roger's private wine cellar. But that's
not all…After your main course, head over to Massimo and
Giselle's home for some very special confections to end a perfect
evening.

Menu to be determined.

Third Saturday night in June

Minimum Bid: $350 per couple.

~ ~ ~

$\mathcal{L}$ izbet had spent hours getting ready for this evening. Her ash blonde hair had been freshly cut and styled at the José Eber salon this morning. While at the salon, she had also decided to let the girls do her makeup since she still had enough time after her manicure and pedicure appointments. The Saks Fifth Avenue tag on her new black-and-white Dior dress had been snipped off just one hour ago when she decided that she would definitely keep this number. Grant told her that he thought it looked especially beautiful on her. (Lizbet thought he must be up to something.) She added some Mikimoto pearls with diamond rondelles and a matching set of pearl and diamond earrings. Simple but elegant.

Tonight should be a huge success. Lizbet had gently persuaded many of her fellow Bronxville Book Club members to bid on this particular item, a sumptuous dinner that promised good food, fine wine, and highly entertaining company. The best part was, she didn't have to worry if anyone had read the book! Her book club ladies were a great group, but reading the monthly book selection was not their strong suit. But she knew they liked terrific food, wine and company, and this evening had all those ingredients in abundant supply. It would be a bit different than the usual book club meetings, since the husbands or significant others would be joining them, but that should make it even more fun. There would also be some new blood since Lizbet had convinced her new neighbor, Morgan Braithwaite, to add his name to the list for this event. Everyone was very curious to get to know his wife, Brooke.

Lizbet stepped over to the Chippendale Ladies Writing Desk in the corner of her bedroom suite and reviewed the neatly typed list of those who were scheduled to attend the dinner. As Grant fastened his Longmire cuff links sporting the family crest, she read off the names and gave him a brief reminder about each of the couples.

"You know our hosts and hostesses, Roger and Sarah, and Massimo and Giselle." As she extended her arm to Grant so he could fasten the clasp on her diamond tennis bracelet, Lizbet continued. "Roger was just promoted to the Director of Cardiology at Westchester Medical. And now that Sarah finally "retired" from her job at the bank, I'm sure she would be just delighted to join some of my committees to fill up her days. Her daughter is going to Georgetown next year, and her son Dylan will be going into High School. I'll have to take her aside at dinner tonight and get her signed up for some interesting activities."

Lizbet barely paused before commenting on the Ceravalos. "You've met Giselle and Massimo a few times. Remember when we hosted that cocktail party for the Republican Party candidates? You may not have noticed her, but Giselle was the one all the men were buzzing around."

Grant certainly did remember.

"The Ceravalos volunteered to have everyone over to their house for dessert. Aren't they just the most stunning couple in town? Massimo used to model for those romance novel covers, ripping the bodices off nubile young maidens. Not that I ever read any of them. But he still looks pretty good, don't you think? I just saw his picture in the latest Brooks Brothers ad in the *New York Times*. He's still as handsome as ever."

Grant couldn't remember speaking more than two words to Massimo, but he wouldn't mind speaking with Giselle this evening. She certainly was a beautiful woman.

"And it's a good thing I like Giselle or I would absolutely hate her! I know I take good care of myself, too, but I wish I had her height and those long legs. Did you know that Massimo and Giselle met during a photo shoot in Manhattan? He was posing for the cover of the latest Barbara Cartland novel, and she was in town working on a lingerie layout for Vogue."

Grant adjusted his Burberry Classic Stripe tie and turned toward his closet to grab a belt as Lizbet chattered on. "Giselle was *so* fortunate that she was able to get involved with the design end of the business. You know that female models just aren't "viable" when they reach a certain age. And she and Massimo have those two precious young daughters, Hannah and Lily, who are as pretty as their mother. Grant, doesn't it seem like only yesterday that our Whitney was in elementary school? And now here we are preparing her college applications."

Grant smiled at the mention of his daughter as Lizbet carried the guest list over to the large picture window and reviewed the names of the other couples who were expected to attend the dinner. Brooke and Morgan headed the list.

Grant didn't need to be reminded that Brooke and Morgan had just moved into the old DuPont house next door to them. He and Morgan had already played golf on several occasions and spent hours debating the nuances of the various courses they had both played all over the world. Grant insisted that St. Andrews was the golf experience of a lifetime, while Morgan pined for the days he could play the Monterey Peninsula at Pebble Beach most weekends. Both had played in numerous member/guest tournaments with other giants of industry at some of the most prestigious private clubs in the United States. Morgan had recently played as part of a foursome with Bill Gates at the Stillwater Cover Golfing Society in Northern California, while Grant had recently golfed with Warren Buffett at the Omaha Country Club. Both had played with The Donald at Winged Foot, yet neither had committed to the $300,000 plus membership deposit for Trump's own private golf club in Westchester.

Before Grant could be sidetracked by thoughts of his beloved golf courses, Lizbet moved on to the next couple on the list and gave Grant a brief update. "Kathryn and her "friend" Trip will be there. Given Kathryn's age, it feels so silly to call Trip Kathryn's "boy"friend. I think he's a partner at one of those big consulting firms in Manhattan. Grant, you've met him before—he used to be married to Claire Rothschild. Remember when Claire and I headed up that *Trails for Treasure* program for the Junior League?"

Without waiting for a response from Grant, Lizbet rambled on about her friend Kathryn. "Brooke and Morgan already know Kathryn since she was the real estate agent who represented the DuPont estate. Kathryn seems to be doing quite well since her divorce from David. At least she had the good sense to get that barracuda lawyer and hold onto that gorgeous house on Masterton and the ski lodge in Vail. Hopefully she also gets a nice fat alimony check every month to go with the properties."

Lizbet sighed when she came to the names of Carole and Andrew Grayson. "I can't say I really like Carole, and you know how I can get along with just about anyone, isn't that right? But she recently married Andrew, so of course we need to include her in our activities. It's a good thing his ex-wife—and my dear friend Alexandra—didn't sign up for tonight's dinner. Alexandra is living with her new husband in that fabulous Victorian on Sunset and Paradise, while Carole and Andrew are crammed into a Lilliputian apartment on Sagamore. To make matters worse, Andrew and Alexandra's two teen-aged daughters—what are their names?—are not at all happy to have Carole as their stepmother. Carole told me she wants her own children with Andrew, but you know Grant, he is fifteen years older than she is, and he just doesn't want to go down that road again. He works so hard to support both families, and I'm not sure Carole really appreciates him."

Grant told Lizbet that since Andrew was an entertainment attorney, he and Morgan should have something in common. Hopefully none of Andrew's clients had ever sued GOM or any of their superstar clients.

Lizbet turned and brushed an imaginary piece of lint off her dress as she checked her reflection in the full-length Cheval mirror. "Francesca and Robert are planning to attend. Whitney never had Francesca as a teacher, since she took French and Latin, and Francesca teaches only Spanish at the Middle School. She's *very* nice. You can't get her to say a mean word about anyone. Not that I've tried, of course. The kids say she looks just like Catherine Zeta Jones. Do you think so, too, Grant?"

Grant paused as he combed his silver-flecked hair and looked over at his wife. "Oh, no Lizzie, I am not going there."

"Anyway, she'll be there with her husband Robert. He owns one of those head-hunting firms, but don't call it that or you'll insult him. I think the proper term is *executive search and consulting*. Whatever. His business must be doing better if they could afford to bid on this dinner. Like us, they only have one child. Their son must be very bright—he's not at Yale, but he did get into M.I.T."

Lizbet ran her perfectly-manicured index finger down the guest list and stopped at the names of a couple that had cancelled their participation. "You probably don't remember Hillary and Bradford. Hillary was that really thin woman who always baked a ton of goodies for the Memorial Day Bake Sale."

Grant interrupted. "Lizbet, thin describes more than half of your friends. I have absolutely no idea who you're talking about."

"You most certainly do know who Hillary is...or was. She was always running down at the track. She was too thin, if you ask me."

Grant was astonished. "If you say someone is too thin, she must have been almost invisible."

Lizbet gave Grant a withering look. "Hillary and Brad are getting a divorce. It really doesn't surprise me. But I guess we won't be seeing much of her anymore, now that they're not together. It's too messy when couples split up, don't you think? It makes it so hard to plan dinner parties and things. It's very hard on the hostess."

With no comment forthcoming from Grant, Lizbet moved on. "Chelsea and Ted are planning to come. Chelsea was kind enough to auction off her landscape consulting services and Morgan won! Remind me to ask her about the Ginkgo Tree in the back that you don't like. Maybe she has some new ideas for us. I'm thinking of taking her advanced gardening course at the Bronxville Adult School that she teaches in the fall, *if* I have the time. I will be so busy with my, I mean Whitney's, senior year."

Grant reached for his wallet and keys atop the valet and asked Lizbet if she were almost ready. "Yes, I'm ready. I just need to grab my purse." As she headed into her walk-in closet, Grant could hear her talking about her friend Madison. "Madison and John will be there, but she said they had a cocktail party they had to go to first. Did you see Madison on the last School Board meeting that was on cable? Besides having such a demanding full-time job, she manages to give so much of her time to the school. Did you know it was through her work with Tiffany's that we were able to arrange the tour we auctioned off? Not that I understand these things very well, but Madison told me she was part of the team that handled Tiffany's IPO, or whatever you call it."

Grant started to explain that "IPO means their initial public offering which…"

Lizbet interrupted. "Yes, that's all very interesting—she must be very bright. But she could use a little help with her wardrobe. If only she would spend just a little more time coordinating her accessories. I should probably offer to help her. I'm sure she'd be grateful that I want to share my fashion advice. I'd do it tactfully, of course." Lizbet paused. "And John is such a dear. Now remember to pay careful attention when the subject of college inevitably comes up. Their son Cole is a senior and rumor has it that he applied to several of the Ivies, including Yale. See if you can find out if John and Madison have an "in" on the Yale Admissions Committee. But don't you dare let slip about anyone we have spoken to on Whitney's behalf."

Lizbet emerged from the closet with her Marc Jacobs clutch and led the way down the winding staircase. In the foyer, they said good night to Mrs. McGrath and reminded her to make sure that Whitney showed her the clothes she needed ironed and packed for her upcoming trip to Paris.

The Smiths took Grant's Porsche 911 Carrera 4S since he never missed an opportunity to take his pride and joy out for a drive. He gently steered the car out of the spacious garage and turned toward the Hilltop, where Roger and Sarah had recently moved. As they approached Valley Road, they could see the lights blazing at the Hamiltons. Judging by the number of cars lining the surrounding cobblestone streets, it appeared that quite a few couples had already arrived.

At the chimes, the front door was opened by a lovely young college girl in an A-line black skirt and white blouse with three-quarter length sleeves. The demure eighteen-year-old ushered the new arrivals through a generous archway towards the main drawing room. Once inside the understated yet elegant salon, Lizbet's eye was drawn upward to the ornate molding and crystal chandelier that radiated a warm glow upon the assembled guests. As Lizbet and Grant approached the other couples, a tall young man in black pants and crisp white shirt offered them a cocktail from a sterling silver Tiffany tray. Another pretty young lady offered them petite crab cakes with fresh chive remoulade sauce.

Roger, their host, was over by a side table that held a hand-blown crystal caviar server atop a matching bowl of shaved ice. As he sampled a serving of caviar on thick toast points, Roger welcomed Lizbet and Grant.

Lizbet pecked Roger on the cheek. "How is our favorite cardiologist?" Roger shook Grant's hand as he responded that he was just splendid. As the Director of the Department of Medicine at the Westchester Cardiology Center, Roger was quite a busy man. Grant asked him how things were going at the Center.

"As long as people keep smoking and overeating, I'll have a job for life."

"Anything new you're working on?"

"Some wonderful research is happening. Some of my colleagues have discovered how to facilitate the regeneration of heart cells. When I went to medical school, we were taught that a man had only a finite number of cells, but my younger colleagues are doing some brilliant work that could lead to much better mortality rates for victims of heart disease."

Lizbet asked, "I've always wondered what the difference is between cardiac arrest and a heart attack. Aren't they the same thing?"

"Not really. A heart attack means that you have a blockage in an artery that goes to your heart. If the heart stops as a result, the patient is in cardiac arrest."

Sarah joined them and told them that as fascinating as Roger's favorite topic was, everyone needed to move into the dining room for dinner.

The table setting was exquisite. Atop a cream damask table cloth was plain Tiffany bone china and sterling flatware. Alongside each plate was lead-crystal stemware by Riedel. Roger was a wine connoisseur who insisted that different glasses be used to enhance the characteristics of the different wine varietals.

At each guest's place setting was an elegant menu printed on the tissue-thin parchment. Sarah had prevailed upon Paisley, the owner of *Kensington Paper*, to special order the engraved menus and the invitations each guest had received.

Appetizer

New England Clam Chowder ~ Creamy rich and loaded with native clams

Five Onion Bisque—Hamilton's own signature soup with pureed carmelized shallots, red onion, sweet onion, scallions, & leeks deglazed with California Chardonnay

Salad

Watercress & Baby Greens ~ Blend of organically grown Baby Greens, Belgian Endive & Watercress dressed with a Balsamic Vinaigrette.

Caesar Salad ~ Whole Romaine heart leaves tossed in classic dressing, presented with garlic crouton wafer

Main Course

Lobster Beggar's Purse ~ Fresh Maine lobster meat sautéed in a light shallot and Chablis crème then wrapped in a crepe and complimented with a saffron crème & American caviar.

Aged Tenderloin ~ beef tenderloin over caramelized purple onions & a French morel cabernet reduction demiglace, served with roasted turned potatoes and a bouquet of baby vegetables.

Selection of fine wines

1997 Louis Jadot, Puligny Montrachet, France
1998 Mouton Rothschild, Pauillac
1999 Clos L'Eglise, Pomerol

Sarah had carefully arranged the seating so that the couples wouldn't be seated next to each other, thereby giving them an opportunity to converse with some of their neighbors whom they didn't see every day. Roger and Sarah sat at either end of the table, with their guests flanking them. To Roger's left were Giselle, Trip, Chelsea, Robert, Madison, Grant, Ted and Lizbet. To Sarah's left were John, Francesca, Morgan, Andrew, Brooke, Carole, Massimo and Kathryn. As each diner took his or her place, conversations sprang up.

Andrew asked Morgan what he thought of the new mega-star dubbed "Tween Queen" by *Vanity Fair*. Morgan knew Andrew was talking about the ubiquitous Hilary Duff, known to his daughters as Lizzie McGuire. Morgan told Andrew he wished they had a Hilary at GOM. "Hilary is a one-person media conglomerate. She has a top-rated Disney show, a movie that grossed over $50 million before it even hit the international market, a music CD that immediately went platinum, a series of books based on her Disney character that sold over 2 million copies, a TV pilot for the networks, a clothing line, games, dolls, school supplies, and who knows what else."

Andrew commiserated that his entertainment law practice could use a few clients like Hilary as well. His team of lawyers had missed out on representing the latest winner of the American Idol competition, but his firm was in negotiations to represent the promising runner-up. He asked Morgan what GOM was doing to keep an eye on the new legal version of Napster, the original file-sharing service that had wreaked havoc in the music industry.

"We're backing several of the new sites to get people to start paying for songs instead of tapping into the demon spawn descendants of Napster." He told Andrew he had even caught Spencer, his own flesh and blood, logging onto KaZaA and Morpheus to swap pirated songs for free. "Spencer lost so many privileges for that transgression that I can guarantee he won't be doing that again any time soon."

Andrew asked hadn't the music companies been trying for years to create sites where customers would pay to "rent" the songs?

"Yes, but we made the mistake of charging monthly fees that customers were just not willing to pay. The fees are gone, and the strategy is to get the fans to pay 99 cents for a song, just as if they were buying a single at Tower Records. Once they've downloaded the track, they can use it any way they want—for their own personal use, *not* the use of every close personal friend who accesses KaZaA!"

Andrew explained how his legal firm's internet practice had grown tremendously over the last few years. He knew that many people thought that the whole music industry was evil and deserved to lose money. "Most consumers think CDs are much too expensive, and why buy the cow when you can get the milk for free?" He told Morgan, "My partner's son was busted at college. He was one of the unlucky ones who became part of a lawsuit by the recording companies against users of file-sharing programs."

Morgan nodded vigorously. "How many parents do you know who think it's no big deal? Even lawyers in your field who know that internet music sharing is a copyright violation allow their own kids to do it. Can you tell me how it is that normally law-abiding citizens think it's just fine to get music for nothing?"

Andrew sidestepped the issue and asked for more specifics on how the music companies were tackling the issue of the high cost of CDs. Morgan told him that a lot of labels were slashing the suggested retail price of most CDs. He acknowledged that they needed to step outside the box and rethink the whole strategy if they were going to compete with "free." His executives were challenged to come up with more creative ways of pricing a new CD and calculating royalties. They were struggling to reach a consensus on how much the record companies should dictate what customers can do with the music once they buy it.

Andrew advised Morgan not to worry. "Graying boomers are coming to the rescue."

Morgan knew exactly what he was talking about. Rod Stewart, Barbra Streisand, the Divine Miss M, and Elvis were still going strong and selling to that golden market niche—affluent boomers who know what a vinyl LP was and expected to actually pay for their music. Morgan laughed, "Our overpaid marketing geniuses earn their bonuses by thinking up ways to repackage yet another collection of the Beatles' greatest hits to boomers who wouldn't dream of sharing music on the internet."

"Brooke wouldn't know how to file-share the oldies if her life depended on it."

"Carole wouldn't either, but then again, sharing isn't something that comes naturally to her."

Morgan laughed. "My crack team of strategists has begun airing spots for some of our older artists on network TV and CNN. It's having surprising success. *Attention Kmart shoppers, Elvis is in Aisle 4.*"

Carole and Brooke overheard the conversation but ignored the crack about their file-sharing abilities. Carole was more interested in finding out from Brooke if a celebrity fundraising event was something Morgan could be cajoled into chairing. Brooke was polite but noncommittal. She switched the conversation to the current activities Carole was organizing. "Kathryn tells me you're working with a number of children's charity events these days."

"Yes, it's been very rewarding. We just did a carnival at Westchester Medical that Roger spearheaded. He pulled in a lot of the big donors from Chappaqua, Bedford and Scarsdale. It was a huge success in more ways than one. Not only did we raise much-needed funds for the new children's wing, but we also brought a lot of smiles to kids who've been through a lot."

Brooke lowered her fork and picked up her wine glass. "It sounds to me as though you really like children. I understand you spend a lot of time with Andrew's two daughters."

Carole nodded. "It's funny. I know I wouldn't win any stepmother-of-the-year contests. Even if nominated, Mackenzie and Courtney would boycott the awards ceremony! But I know I'd be a good mother. I just have to convince Andrew. He feels that another baby would be too much for us to handle, but I haven't given up."

Brooke looked at Carole with genuine empathy. "I'm sure it will work out for the best. Even if you don't have children of your own, try to enjoy the girls. Don't you remember what it was like to be a teenage girl? I wouldn't go through it again for anything in the world."

Carole agreed. "You know, I never really thought of it like that. I guess I was too wrapped up in my own problems with Andrew and his ex-wife, Alexandra, to look at it from the girls' point of view."

Nearby, Francesca and John were quietly discussing the goings on at the Bronxville School. John was quite delighted that the major construction woes were now behind them so that Madison could focus on the more strategic issues she wanted to tackle as a School Board Member.

Francesca praised John for his work on the Bronxville School Foundation. As a Spanish teacher, she welcomed the new audio/visual equipment they had provided for her students. She was also grateful for the expanded opportunities for staff development that she hoped to put to good use in the classroom.

John asked how Francesca's son, Nicolas, was faring in his senior year at M.I.T. She visibly brightened as she recounted what Nicholas planned to do upon graduation. "He is so excited about his work on this new tracking and identification system that he says will revolutionize how stores manage their inventory. I think it's called RFID. He told me I am already using a version of it because E-Z Pass uses this radio frequency identification. He said category killers like Walmart are demanding that their suppliers use these radio frequency tags on everything they deliver to their warehouses."

John was intrigued. "Is he thinking of going to work for Walmart?"

"No, he wants to work for the companies that make the components, hopefully Intel, IBM, or Microsoft. Personally, I'm hoping he'll stay on the East Coast, but it's a very real possibility that he'll be relocating 3,000 miles away. How about Cole, where does he stand with his college applications?"

"He's narrowed down his choices. He really wants either Princeton or Yale. I think he's got a good shot at both, but he needs to pick a few safety schools. We're planning a few more college tours."

Francesca dabbed her lips with her linen napkin. "I actually enjoyed the college process."

John almost choked. "You're kidding me, right?"

"No, really. I know it's stressful. But think about all the time you get to spend together as you go from college to college. Treasure it, John. The clock is ticking and you won't have too many of these kinds of opportunities in the future."

Further down the table, Kathryn and Massimo looked deep in conversation. If anyone had been listening in, they would have been treated to Massimo's update on Kathryn's former Manny, Carlo.

Kathryn's blue eyes were blazing. She had just learned that all the time Carlo was living with her and "taking care of Pryce," the hottest clubs in Manhattan had been paying him as well—simply to look good! He got $200, free vodka and cranberry, and a VIP table to fill with his equally good-looking friends. As if it weren't bad enough that he was keeping this part-time "job" from her, according to Massimo, Carlo also had been seen leaving various clubs with no fewer than a dozen different women. Kathryn got even angrier as she remembered Carlo's repeated excuses that he needed to visit his elderly aunt in Brooklyn. Why, that…She could wring Carlo's neck. She looked at Massimo, "And they say women are gold diggers? Why didn't you or Giselle ever tell me?"

"Please, Kathryn, don't mention a word of this to Giselle. I haven't shared this with her."

"Why not?"

Massimo looked sheepish. "Let's just say that I would have a lot of explaining to do as to what I was doing at all those clubs in the first place."

Kathryn raised her wineglass and her eyebrows.

At the other end of the table, Sarah was chatting with Lizbet. Lizbet asked Sarah how she liked living in her new house.

"I love it. I've always had my eye on this house, and when Kathryn told us it was coming on the market, Roger and I jumped at it. The good thing is that now I have more time to devote to getting things set up the way we like them."

"So then I take it you haven't had time to train for the marathon or read all those books that you wanted to finish once you retired from the corporate world?"

"No, but I did get to organize Dylan's and Ruthann's baby pictures. With Ruthann heading off to Georgetown in a few months, it was something I wanted to make sure I accomplished. I know I'll be shedding many a tear as I thumb through the albums during her first semester away from home."

Lizbet told her she knew just what she meant. She didn't mention that the picture she fantasized about organizing was a portrait of Whitney's Yale-educated husband to be hung in the Main Lounge of the New York Yale Club.

Lizbet asked if now that Sarah was settled into to her house, she needed some fun committees to fill her days and take her mind off Ruthann's departure.

Sarah shook her head. "Actually, I've accepted some part-time consulting assignments some former colleagues approached me about."

"Why on earth would you do that?"

Sarah didn't hesitate. "I'm my own boss, and I'm doing something I love, on my own timeframes."

Lizbet could not imagine what could be so interesting that Sarah would want to work, even if it was part-time.

"Friends of mine started this business to tutor executives who never quite had the time or the inclination to learn how to use computers themselves. For some, they were afraid of technology; others had "people" who used the computer for them. Well, as we all know, the world is changing and computers are an unavoidable part of our world."

Lizbet couldn't understand what was wrong with having "people" continue to use the computer for them.

"I enjoy doing it, and the $300 an hour does come in handy for the extras Ruthann will need while she's living in Washington. I couldn't say

No, and actually, I'm glad I said *Yes*. I set my own hours and I get to keep my toe in the water in case I ever want to go back full time."

Lizbet looked very disappointed.

Sarah hastened to reassure her. "Don't worry, I'll still help with your committees. Think about which one you need the most help with, and sign me up."

Lizbet perked up and immediately launched into a detailed description of the hundreds of plans she had for the upcoming year.

To Lizbet's right, Grant and Ted were discussing their favorite topic. Cars.

In his firm, patrician manner, Grant asked Ted if that was his Phantom parked at the front of the driveway.

Ted responded that it most definitely was his new baby. He had just picked it up last week.

Grant wasn't surprised Ted had chosen the Phantom, but he couldn't resist a little dig. "You always said you'd never buy anything other than a Mercedes for your own personal car…they were the best…no one could touch them for looks and performance. What made you change?"

Ted shrugged. "I couldn't decide between the Maybach and the Phantom. Yeah, I've always been a Mercedes man, but the Maybach just didn't give me the visual impact I wanted. And with a starting price of $325,000, believe me, I wanted visual impact."

Grant agreed. "Right, at that sticker price, it's not as if you need to worry about how many miles per gallon you get."

Ted raved about his Phantom. "It drives like a dream. It maneuvers well even in Manhattan traffic."

Grant chuckled. "But it doesn't have the Champagne refrigerator that the Maybach has."

"That may be true, but the "Flying Lady" on the hood goes into hiding at the touch of a button. And hubcaps are filled with liquid and rotate independently of the wheels. Did you notice that the RR logo in the center is always in an upright position? Check it out when we go outside later."

Grant wasn't convinced. "I'll never give up my Porsche, no matter how many jokes are made about it being the prescribed treatment for a midlife crisis. Although you won't see me driving that new S.U.V. they came out with. It's powerful and responsive, but at the end of the day, it's still an S.U.V. If you want visual impact, don't pick that baby. At this stage of the game, I don't want a practical Porsche. That's an oxymoron as far as I'm concerned."

Ted wanted to change the subject. "How come you weren't at the C.E.O. Academy seminar last month? Didn't your buddies at Goldman or Weil, Gotshal & Manges try to talk you into leading one of the sessions on corporate leadership or ethics in the post-Enron era?"

Grant sipped his wine. "Actually, I wasn't approached this year." He stared at a Monet on a distant wall. "I'm sure the organizers were just being overly cautious and didn't ask anyone who might have had even a passing relationship with Dennis Kozlowski. He and I weren't good friends, but our paths have crossed over the years."

Ted was surprised. "I didn't realize you knew him personally."

Grant gave a short laugh. "Unfortunately I knew him well enough to have been invited to that fateful party for his second wife's birthday. Thank God Lizbet never cared for Karen, so she declined the invitation on our behalf with our deepest regrets."

While Ted and Grant continued their conversation about former, current, and potential future CEO's they both knew, Madison was asking Robert how the recruiting business was faring these days. Robert was actually more optimistic than he had been of late. Raising his glass of wine, he commented, "As you know all too well, the last few years have been absolutely horrendous. The recent economic news has been almost all good lately, but let's not fool ourselves. Despite recent employment gains, the U.S. economy employs almost 3 million fewer people now than it did when the recession started. Notwithstanding this recent job spurt, my clients tell me that their companies are demanding—and achieving—much more work output from fewer employees. Economists call this the new "normal." Friends of mine who are still unemployed or have been forced to accept lower-paying jobs call it "depressing."

Madison agreed. "As I'm sure your son, Nicholas, makes you painfully aware, technology is revolutionizing how we do business. Although some analysts bemoan what will happen when the baby-boom generation retires and causes a labor shortage in the U.S., let's face it. A lot of jobs are moving overseas to India, China, Russia and the Phillipines."

Robert shook his head ruefully. "It's true. The pundits have already coined a new name for it—offshoring. Companies like Dell and Netgear can outsource programming and call center operations and realize huge gains in productivity and labor costs. They can pay a programmer in India $6 an hour, or pay the same worker $60 in the U.S. As if that weren't enough, they also get the added benefit of improved customer service by having staff in time zones around the world. Need your computer fixed at 3:00 in the morning? No problem. We are a 24/7 society. But there are other industries that are actually adding jobs—health care, real estate, and education. I'm currently handling the staffing for a number of different health care companies, but most of those jobs don't pay as well as the finance and tech jobs that have disappeared during the last few years. At least I'm encouraged that in the future there will be a lot of high-paying jobs created in industries we haven't even dreamed of yet, but I need to pay Nicholas' college bills today."

As Robert and Madison continued their conversation, Chelsea turned to Trip. "I'm so glad they seated us together. I haven't seen you in ages. How have you been?"

Trip had an engaging smile. "Great. Since my divorce from Claire I don't get to see as many of our old friends as often. But now that I'm seeing Kathryn, I seem to be getting back in the swing of things."

Chelsea asked, "Are you living in Westchester again?"

Trip explained, "I spend Monday through Friday at my apartment on the upper East Side, but I just bought a place on Pondfield Road over by

Village Hall. It's convenient for when I have my son, Jake, stay with me for the weekend."

"Business good?"

Trip nodded. "Surprisingly good. I've been involved in a number of long-term consulting projects that keep me busy. Most of my clients are still in the Wall Street area, but a few have relocated uptown. I still can't get over the change in the Times Square area since Disney moved into the neighborhood. When my friends and I were teenagers, we'd take the train in from Bronxville to check out the seedy side of Manhattan. What a change."

Chelsea agreed wholeheartedly. "Don't I know it. I get over to that side of town when I'm working with a new group that one of my colleagues started, the New York City Beautification Council."

"You should be very proud of your work in the city. When I come out of Grand Central I always admire what groups like yours have accomplished. Do you want me to introduce you to some folks involved in other parts of the city who are interested in starting similar projects?"

Chelsea didn't hesitate for a minute. "Please, No! I hardly have time for what I'm committed to right now. I just wish I could clone myself. There's so much I want to do, but I am just spread too thin. Besides consulting in the city, I'm very lucky that my landscaping business in Westchester is thriving. And Michael and Lucas need more time and attention. Their grandfather helps out, but I want to be around more. That was one of the reasons I chose to start a business out of my home. I have to keep reminding myself of that whenever I'm tempted to get involved in a new project elsewhere."

Trip understood. "Well, if you every change your mind…"

The meal was winding down. The waiter must have missed Roger's signal not to refill Giselle's wine glass. She picked up the delicate, mouth-blown crystal goblet and gestured wildly as she spoke to Roger. "Didn't I hear you say these glasses direct the flow of air and liquid to the right taste receptors? Well, you were soooo right. My taste receptors are very happy right now."

Giselle leaned closer to Roger. "Speaking of receptors, Dr. Roger, did you see that headline in the Wall Street Journal about underwear being able to detect heart abnormalities?"

Roger laughed heartily.

"I'm serious Roger. The Dutch have actually figured out a way to design underwear that can sense heart-rhythms and even call for the ambulance."

Roger had missed that bit of research, but he did ask Giselle if she had also read the latest findings that moderate drinking—not more than two drinks a day for men and one a day for women—was associated with a lower risk for heart attacks. Instead of answering, she took a sip of Chardonnay as Roger continued. "Actually, red wine may even provide an extra advantage because it contains flavanoids, which my research colleagues assure me helps prevent heart disease."

Seemingly oblivious to the fact that Roger had even spoken, Giselle babbled on. "I read that you can sew these chips into bras and shorts to monitor the heart signals, and I want to be the first to design the lifesaving lingerie collection."

Giselle took a gulp of wine. "And speaking of being first, one of my design partners on the West Coast told me about this new plastic surgery salon in Beverly Hills, right near Chanel. For only $5,000 you can get a face lift or tummy tuck without having to go to a hospital. Maybe I can set up a little boutique there to sell fabulous new garments for the women to buy once their procedures are over. Buying something feminine always makes me feel better."

Roger started to respond but Giselle interrupted. "I keep in shape with yoga, but I have been thinking about a face lift. These models I'm around all the time look so damn young, not a wrinkle or sag anywhere."

Giselle leaned closer to Roger and confided in a conspiratorial whisper, "Professionally speaking, Doctor, I'm sure you've noticed how well my surgery turned out."

"I'm not sure what…"

She leaned in closer, and with her eyes, directed his gaze to her chest.

Roger coughed and took a sip of wine.

"Do you think they did a good job?"

Roger signaled for the waiter to clear the plates.

Sarah rose and asked everyone to adjourn to the living room. It was time to get ready for their very special dessert.

As everyone moved into the spacious living room for an after-dinner cordial, several of the men surreptitiously pleaded with their wives to call it a night. Through clenched jaw, Grant asked Lizbet if it were really necessary for them to head over to Giselle's for dessert.

Lizbet glared at Grant. She wouldn't hear of going home. Her body language made it quite clear that there would be no further discussion.

Once all were assembled in the living room sipping their brandies, Sarah announced that their transportation would arrive shortly. Most of the guests were surprised, as they had planned to drive their own cars the short distance to Giselle and Massimo's. But as they filed outside, they were pleased to see the brand new fleet of London-style cabs lined up in the circular driveway outside the house.

Lizbet beamed at how delighted everyone was with this surprise. These new taxis were authentic black cabs that the local livery company had purchased from an entrepreneur who imported about 125 of the British cars into the United States.

The first cab, with its signature golden crown on the roof, pulled up to the front door. As the driver stepped out to open the back door, Roger directed the first two couples to hop into the roomy passenger compartment. With the traditional back-facing, fold-up jump seats, four people fit with room to spare. Once their guests were taken care of, Sarah and Roger shuffled into the last cab and followed the procession to the Ceravalos. Giselle and Massimo had left a few minutes earlier so that Giselle could get things ready for the finale of the evening.

Lizbet, Grant, Morgan and Brooke were in the lead taxi. Morgan and Grant had gallantly taken the jump seats so that their wives could have the comfortable back seat. They continued their good-natured grumbling about wanting to call it a night, but were surprised when Lizbet suddenly agreed that maybe Grant was right. Was she really saying that it was getting late, and they should only stay a minute to say goodnight before heading home?

Grant and Morgan looked at each other quizzically but were not about to question why Lizbet had changed her mind. They were ready to retrieve their cars and turn in for the evening. Before they could say a word, the driver of the taxi hopped out and helped the ladies alight. As Morgan and Grant followed, it was only then that they realized why the sudden change of heart.

Waiting at the front door was Massimo, who had gotten into the spirit of serving dessert in style by donning a starched white bistro apron. At his side, Giselle had changed into a skimpy French maid outfit topped with a crisp white cap and frilly apron.

As Lizbet tugged at his sleeve to say their goodnights, Grant said, "Nonsense, Lizbet. Who said anything about turning in early? The night is young, and besides, all of a sudden I'm in the mood for some dessert…perhaps a nice tart."

"Speak the truth, but leave immediately after."

Slovenian Proverb

Chapter 4

Happy Birthday!

~~~

Francesca Walker, your children's favorite Middle School Spanish teacher, will keep your child and ten special friends spellbound at a truly unusual birthday party. She will introduce your child to the favorite games of yore…pin the tail on the donkey; musical chairs; hot potato, and many, many more.

Minimum Bid: $500

~~~

*F*rancesca arrived at the Braithwaite home exactly thirty minutes before the guests were scheduled to arrive. Lizbet's daughter Whitney had volunteered to help out and should be there any minute. Francesca's son Nicholas was home from M.I.T. and he, too, had offered his services. While he genuinely wanted to help, he also was looking forward to seeing the kids' reactions to the party. He could imagine their shock when they realized there would be no travelling petting zoo, no team of hair stylists and make-up artists to make them look glamorous, and no Broadway entertainers to put on a private show. Jaded by parties that raised the bar to ridiculous heights, these little girls were in for a birthday party experience unlike any they had enjoyed before.

Nicholas unloaded the car while Francesca sought out Brooke and her daughter Jayne, the birthday girl. Jayne was in the sunroom playing with the new kitten she had received for her birthday. As Francesca approached, Jayne jumped up and hid behind her mother's legs. Francesca smiled and wished her *Feliz Cumpleaños* as she handed her a gaily wrapped box. Jayne looked at Brooke, who nodded and encouraged her to accept the gift and say thank you.

Although Brooke had told Jayne she couldn't open her presents until after the party was over, Jayne pleaded to open just this one.

Brooke agreed she could open just one, and Jayne carefully undid the wrapping, making the moment last as long as possible.

Francesca knew that children this age were quite honest in their reactions as they hadn't yet learned the "art" of exclaiming over a gift that disappointed.

Jayne had no need to pretend. She loved the porcelain tea set and *Miss Spider's Tea Party* book Francesca had selected for her. Francesca always made sure to buy children gifts that required only an imagination instead of 4 "C" batteries.

As the kitten played among the discarded wrappings, Francesca bent down and asked Jayne what she had named the kitten.

"Pickles."

Francesca smiled. "That's a wonderful name. I'm sure he will love his new home."

Jayne picked up her tiny kitten and stroked his soft grey fur.

Francesca moved closer. "May I touch him?"

Nodding her head in agreement, Jayne removed her hand so that Francesca could pet Pickles.

"He is purring. He must be very happy." After a short time, Francesca asked, "Do you think Pickles would be okay in here while we go outside and see what Nicholas has in the box he's bringing into the yard?"

Jayne accepted Francesca's outstretched hand. They opened the side door of the sunroom and walked down the path and through the archway into the back yard. Brooke took the opportunity to go into the kitchen to see if Mariella had finishing decorating the white buttercream sheet cake with pink roses.

Whitney had arrived, and she and Nicholas were hard at work making sure all the decorations were in place. They blew up oodles of purple, yellow and baby blue balloons that they scattered throughout the yard. Jayne and Francesca walked over and helped drape rolls of rainbow-colored crepe paper on two of the large maple trees in the front of the yard. Jayne was already having a great time when she heard the first guests beginning to arrive.

Giselle held Lily's hand as they approached the backyard with several other children and their mothers. After Giselle gave a final adjustment to the crisp purple bow that adorned Lily's soft blonde hair, the little girl ran up to Jayne and proudly handed over a beautifully-wrapped package from *Try & Buy*. Jayne thanked her new friend and together they skipped over to the gift table to add it to the pile that was quickly building as several more little girls streamed into the yard.

Giselle moved slowly to join the other mothers at a table under the shade of the huge dogwood tree. She didn't want to admit it, but the foot surgery she had just suffered through to give her better toe cleavage had not been as easy as she had been led to believe. But she quickly put it out of her mind and smiled broadly at the other mothers. Counting heads, she was surprised there would only be a total of 8 little girls and boys. Giselle had just held Lily's party at the *American Girl Place* in Manhattan. There they insisted on a minimum of 15 girls, but Giselle had more trouble keeping the number of guests under the maximum of 25 allowed. It was well worth the $250 per child since the girls had a meal in the Café, saw a live musical performance, and got to take their dolls to the hair salon. For Jayne's party, Francesca had gently insisted that Brooke follow a tried-and-true rule of inviting only one more than the age of the birthday child.

Two of the other mothers—Abigail and Tricia—were in the middle of a very serious conversation about the placements for the new fifth grade classes. Giselle was especially interested in what they were saying, since her other daughter Hannah had been very upset that she wasn't going to be in a class with any of her friends and was convinced the whole year would be horrible. Giselle thought she knew how to play the game. At the end of fourth grade she had written the letter about the next year's placement and didn't directly ask for a specific teacher. Instead, she simply made sure to use all the right code words so that Hannah would be placed with the teacher who was warm and nurturing. But Hannah was placed with the teacher who had the least tolerance for sensitive girls like Hannah who needed to be treated with extra TLC.

Giselle was shocked to hear these mothers discussing what they called the "copy machine" scandal. When questioned, Abigail explained that a mother of a fourth grader had taken a confidential list of the fifth-grade class placements for the upcoming school year from the copy machine while the secretary wasn't in the office. She then had the nerve to make an appointment with the principal to complain that her daughter wasn't going to be in the "popular" class with the "best" teacher.

Giselle was incredulous. "Did the principal change her daughter's class?"

Tricia shook her head. "No, there would have been anarchy. But I did hear that the mom is appealing the decision to the Superintendent. Trust me, she is not one who is used to taking "no" for an answer."

As Giselle tried to find out who the mystery mom was, Francesca was gathering the children together for their first game. Seven chairs were arranged back-to-back. With fewer chairs than children, a short snippet of music was played while the children moved around the chairs. Nicholas had his back to the group so that when he hit the "Stop" button on his old-fashioned Fisher Price recorder, he was not able to see which children were scrambling for the vacant chairs.

Jayne's friend Victoria didn't find a chair, but Whitney quickly extended her hand and led the little girl to a spot nearby so they could watch the next round. They were soon joined by another little girl, and then another, until only 2 children were left.

When the final song was stopped, the little red-headed girl was victorious. The runner-up ran over and buried her head in her mother's lap. As her mother reassured her that she was right, it wasn't fair, Nicholas came up and knelt down to talk to the little girl. He persuaded her to give the next game a try. As they walked off together, he told her of the many times he had lost a game, but how after a while it didn't really matter if he didn't come in first, since he had so much fun playing the game. She looked perplexed. Nicholas didn't know if his new friend was convinced, but she did jump up enthusiastically when she saw that a game of Musical Statues was about to begin. This time Whitney was operating the recorder. When the music played, the children leaped into frenzied motion dancing and gyrating to the beat. But when the music stopped, everyone had to keep perfectly still. It was amazing to the parents watching how their normally quivering, shaking, jumping children could be as still as a statue at the prospect of winning a 25-cent trinket.

After several rounds, and much giggling, the children were ready for Pass the Orange. Nicholas and Whitney each formed a team of four. Each team stood in a line, one behind the other. Each group was given an orange, which the first person tucked under his or her chin. The orange was then passed to the child behind. When—and if!—the orange reached the last person, that child came to the front of the line and started again.

The winning team was the first one to get their starting person to the front of the line three times.

The oranges rolled in all directions, and the kids had to start over at the front of the line. Boys squirmed at the prospect of touching a girl to pass the orange. Parents shouted enthusiastic encouragement to both teams. At the end of the game, Francesca declared it a tie, much to the delight of all the children.

Sticking with the fruit and vegetable theme, Francesca asked the children to stand in a circle for a game of Hot Potato. Nicolas produced a raw potato and the children passed it around. He turned his back and waited a few minutes before blowing a whistle. The unfortunate holder of the potato gave the potato to the next child and stepped over to join Whitney. As the game progressed, the potato was "passed" in a more and more spirited manner. It was flying through the air by the time only two children were left. When the last whistle blew, Lily had the potato and Jayne was victorious. But when Jayne was presented with her prize, she asked Francesca if she could give it to Lily since she hadn't won any of the games yet. Francesca agreed that was a splendid idea.

The children followed Francesca over to a side area to play Pin the Tail on the Donkey. While the children were occupied, Nicolas and Whitney began preparing a long oblong table with plain white paper and crayons for some creative coloring. As they got the supplies ready, Nicolas asked Whitney how the college search was going.

She groaned, "Not you, too."

Nicholas looked surprised. "Not me too, what?"

Whitney sighed and patiently explained her frustration. "For some reason, the only question anyone ever asks me and my friends anymore is about college. Where am I applying? What were my SAT scores? How many AP courses have I taken? I can't wait for this whole process to be over!" As she set out the crayons, she mused, "Maybe I'll be like Bill Gates, or Ted Turner, or Michael Dell. They never even got a college degree, and I bet no one is asking them about their SAT scores."

Nicholas moved over to her side of the table. "Sorry, Whitney. Especially with the questions I'm getting these days, I guess I should be more sensitive. People want to know where I'm applying for a job, how many interviews have I had, and if I've received any job offers yet. I know people mean well, but I can understand how you just don't want to talk about it all the time."

Whitney relaxed. "Apology accepted." She doodled with the blue crayon while they waited for the children to finish their other game. "Maybe I should go into publishing. Look at how the magazines like *U.S. News & World Report* and *Atlantic Monthly* have created a whole college ranking industry that feeds on the anxieties of people like my parents. You wouldn't believe how upset they got when they saw that Yale tied with M.I.T. for the #3 spot in *U.S. News*, but in *Atlantic Monthly*, M.I.T. was #1 and Yale was a miserable #4!"

Nicholas laughed. "It's not just the parents. Even the colleges are caught up in the whole frenzy. Did you hear about the new $53 million dollar wellness center at the University of Houston? It has a five-story climbing wall."

"I hadn't heard about that one. But I had heard that Colgate sold the naming rights for their climbing wall for $50,000, but please don't tell my mother or you'll give her ideas. She'd probably donate a climbing building to Yale if it would ensure I'd go there."

Nicholas laughed and moved the box that had been emptied of its craft supplies. "Personally, I like the new sports campuses. Ohio State is spending about $140 million on a huge facility that will have kayaking, canoeing, batting cages, and rope courses."

Whitney countered, "I'll take the campuses that now give massages, pedicures and manicures on demand. I heard about some university on the West Coast that has this huge Jacuzzi that can hold 53 of your closest fellow students."

"Amazing. But the Ivies don't have to offer all that stuff. Kids would kill to get into Princeton or Harvard."

"Au contraire," Whitney said as she shook her head. "Cornell is investing almost $300 million in new dorms."

Nicholas shook his head. "I'll bet the new dorms are nicer than any apartment I'll be able to afford in the near future. I'd like to live in the city, but the rents are outrageous."

"New York City? And leave this suburban heaven to become an over-moisturized metrosexual?" Whitney quickly added, "Don't answer that. I think even I'd become a metrosexual to escape suburbia."

With Whitney's help, Nicholas straightened the chairs around the table. "The reality of it is, Whitney, that even the Trustees of schools like Cornell, and the other Ivies, are not just doing it for the students. They have to impress the big donors who get out the checkbook because they want to be associated with such esteemed institutions of higher learning."

"I know. I'm the daughter of that kind of donor."

Nicholas teased her. "I always knew you were an heirhead."

Whitney chased him around the table but he was much too fast for her. He reversed direction and tackled her on the grass. They rolled around laughing until they were out of breath. After a minute, Nicholas got up and reached down to pull Whitney up. "Come on, they're playing Chinese Whispers. Do you remember this game?"

By the time Whitney and Nicholas got to the children, they were already arranged in a circle. Francesca explained the rules of the game to the attentive group. "Someone has to whisper a long sentence or a short poem to the person next to him or her. That person whispers what he or she heard to the next person and so on. Any questions?" After a pause, Francesca announced, "Okay, then, let's begin."

Jayne asked Whitney to sit next to her and start the game. Whitney tried to convince Jayne that it would be more fun if she made up a sentence or a funny poem, but Jayne wouldn't hear of it.

Whitney thought about what to say. She decided to have some fun with it, since no matter what she said, she knew it would be something completely different by the time it reached the eighth child. She quickly composed a silly little poem and leaned over to whisper it to Jayne.

Jayne concentrated hard and then passed on the verse. Whitney was laughing to herself as she tried to imagine how twisted her original ditty would be by the time it reached the last little girl or boy. The parents had slowly been drifting over to hear what all the whispering was about. It finally reached Carolyn, the last little girl. Carolyn was a beautiful child, with wide-set blue eyes and a headful of blonde corkscrew curls. She stood up proudly as Francesca asked her to repeat the sentence for the others.

Carolyn screwed up her face in concentration and began.

"There was a young girl from Bronxville
Whose mommy could not learn to chill
The mother knew best
what the bird in her nest
needed to do to remain in her will."

Whitney cringed. She couldn't believe it. Since when did children this age develop such terrific recall?

Without glancing in Lizbet's direction, Whitney stood up and asked Francesca, "Don't you think this would be a good time for me to take my right foot out of my mouth and use it to play a nice game of Hokey Pokey?"

"A large income is the best recipe for

happiness I ever heard of."

Jane Austen

Chapter 5

Margarita Pool Party

~ ~ ~

Ladies, grab your bikini and pareo, and Gentlemen, grab your surfer shorts, and join new friends for a Margarita pool party you won't soon forget. This special evening will be hosted by Bronxville's very own gourmand, Wyatt Davenport, and his wife Samantha, in their secluded backyard oasis.

Lifeguard included.

Minimum Bid: $300 per family

Children over 5 welcome.

Maximum: Six families

~ ~ ~

*W*yatt Davenport was putting the finishing touches on the hors d'ouevres he had prepared for the outdoor party. He had selected a surf and turf menu that he had recently featured on his local cable cooking show.

Lizbet had cajoled Wyatt, a local culinary celebrity, to cook up something special for the Silent Auction item. Following his success with a series of cookbooks—*Spice Up Your Life; A Wild Thyme with Wyatt; and Seasoning for all Seasons*—and a monthly *"Sage Advice"* column for *Gourmet Magazine,* Wyatt had been offered the host duties on a local cable cooking show, *Cooking with Class.* Many residents also knew Wyatt very well from the cooking and baking seminars he offered at his home to private clients. Lizbet herself had taken advantage of the private sessions, but Grant often wondered if the money would have been better spent if they had sent their housekeeper, Mrs. McGrath, instead.

The Davenports' backyard was specially designed for Wyatt's culinary talents. He had always wanted an outdoor kitchen with an herb garden along the side, and when he and Samantha bought this house, that was the #1 priority on the renovation list. Custom built for the Davenports, the overall effect was incredible. The wood-burning oven served as the focal point amidst all the latest cookware and crockery. It even included an enclosed butler's pantry with a duplicate set of all the supplies he could possibly need for preparing and serving meals outdoors.

The staff Wyatt had hired for the evening was bustling about making sure everything was set. The bartender was organizing a separate table with aged Tequila, Triple Sec, fresh lime wedges, salt, crushed ice and chilled Margarita glasses. Nearby, bottles of Chardonnay, Perrier, and a selection of premium beers stayed deliciously chilled in a large silver container next to the hors d'oeuvres table. To keep it simple, Wyatt had put out a selection of goodies for guests to munch on before the main course. He included golden pastry straws sprinkled with savory Parmesan, four-cheese puff pastry rounds, and open-faced roasted red pepper risotto squares.

Kathryn and her friend Trip were the first to arrive, followed closely by Giselle. Giselle apologized to the Davenports for her husband's absence, but Massimo had a previous commitment he just couldn't escape. Other couples soon entered the backyard, including Claire and James, and Andrea and David. All had brought their children. Although Wyatt had invited the Smiths, Lizbet and Grant wouldn't be joining the party. Even if she didn't have a beach house where they spent the summer, Lizbet would never be one to admit she was in town for the summer. By the time Brooke and Morgan arrived with their girls, Charlotte and Jayne—Spence wouldn't be caught dead at a party with his parents—you could cut the tension with a knife.

The Braithwaites weren't feeling very lucky that they had successfully bid on this Silent Auction item once they realized who the other "winners" were. As hosts, Wyatt and Samantha were trying their best to put everyone at ease. Before Morgan and Brooke had arrived, Samantha had taken Wyatt aside in the kitchen to explain why the families already present were so uncomfortable. She tried to keep it simple, but she could hardly keep it straight herself. "Kathryn and David Chasen are the parents of Pryce. They are no longer married, but they both live in town. Kathryn's dating Trip Thayer, who used to be married to Claire Rothschild. While Claire and Trip were married, they had a son, Jake. They got divorced last year and now Claire is seeing James Witherspoon, who used to be married to Andrea Haverford. Andrea and James have one daughter, Alice. That brings the circle back to the beginning, since Andrea is dating Kathryn's ex, David. To make matters even worse, all three children are in the same fifth grade class at the Bronxville School." Wyatt was not amused. Through clenched teeth, he told Samantha that this was the last time he'd let her talk him into hosting this kind of thing.

It was going to be a long evening.

Brooke and Morgan joined the group scattered around the pool as Samantha made the introductions. Charlotte had met the other children at school and eagerly accepted their invitation to go inside to watch the big screen plasma TV. Despite pleas from their parents to sit outside with them and enjoy the beautiful evening or take a swim, the children continued through the back door and left the adults to their own devices.

As the adults looked at one another, Samantha filled the void. "Well. Brooke, Morgan. Welcome to our home."

Brooke admired Wyatt and Samantha's backyard and marveled at how the neatly-trimmed hedges provided such an effective screen that from the front of the house no one would be able to glimpse this slice of paradise.

Beyond the far end of the pool, in which a pair of large red lobster pool toys were gently drifting, was a dining tent. Through the wide opening of the tent, Brooke could see several round tables set for dinner. White tablecloths were topped with red glassware and plates and a series of candles. A string of red and white lanterns provided festive lighting inside the tent.

Morgan and Brooke excused themselves to get a drink from the outdoor bar, but once they returned they attempted to make conversation with the other couples already seated on plump-cushioned chaise lounges and pool chairs. The designer definitely loved red and white. The cushions on all the chairs were white with lipstick red piping, while the chaise lounge fabrics were just the opposite. Brooke and Morgan accepted hors d'oeuvres from one of Wyatt's assistants and then sat down on two of the empty chairs. Nearby, Kathryn and her ex-husband David were attempting to be civil to each other.

David was asking, "So since you have Pryce for Thanksgiving this year, what are you planning to do?"

Kathryn answered politely, "I thought we might go to London to see my friend, Cynthia. She's been asking us to come for a visit—it's been years since we've been there. I think Pryce would get a real kick out of visiting the barrier between platforms 9 and 10 at Kings Cross Station looking for the Hogwarts' Express."

David agreed. "I think you're right."

Kathryn's eyes widened. "You don't often say that!" She laughed and then asked, "How about you, David? Any plans yet?"

David shrugged. "James has Alice for that holiday, so Andrea and I will probably spend a quiet Thanksgiving at home."

Kathryn was visibly surprised. "No skiing this year?"

David waved his hand in her direction. "Your lawyer negotiated the condo in Vail for you, remember? I haven't bought another place...yet."

Kathryn's color slowly began to rise. "Well, if you think I feel sorry..."

Brooke interrupted, "What is the secret to these cheese sticks?"

Wyatt thanked her with his eyes. "I season the dough first, then cut, roll and twist each one by hand. Then they're baked twice to make them extra crispy. You can try crumbling them into salads too."

Andrea chimed in. "I tried Wyatt's recipe of sage, thyme and marjoram that added just the right balance of seasonings to the dressing for my roast turkey last Thanksgiving."

Wyatt turned to her. "The herbs are also terrific in soups or stews. Don't just save them for Thanksgiving."

Kathryn wasn't finished with David. "So you're actually dating someone old enough to know how to cook?"

David accepted the bait. "Yes, too bad Carlo never learned. Just what was his special talent?"

Kathryn seethed. It was hard for her to imagine that she had once been head-over-heels in love with David. Besides his money, which was still very attractive, she wasn't sure what else he had going for him these days. David would probably still be considered good-looking by a lot of women, but was it his appearance, or was it his money and self confidence that made him good looking? Sure, he was better looking—not to mention taller—than someone like Henry Kissinger. Kathryn always believed it was a man's world. Give a relatively unattractive guy like Kissinger some power and money, and the women lined up.

While Kathryn was lost in thought, Brooke asked Andrea how she and David met. "Oh, we met when I had an assignment to interview him for a freelance article I was doing on Westchester's 10 most eligible bachelors."

Samantha interjected, "Oh, you're a writer?"

Andrea nodded. "Actually, I'm trying to get my writing career started. I do freelance assignments whenever I can get them, but I'd really like to write children's literature. David's been very helpful introducing me to some of his friends who are active in the Manhattan literary scene."

Kathryn whispered to Trip, "She might be blonde and she's definitely ambitious, but she's no Madonna." Trip shot her a warning glance.

Samantha wanted to be encouraging to a new writer. Based on all the people who asked Wyatt for any assistance he could offer, she knew how difficult it was for a first-time author to get published.

David joined the conversation. "You are very talented, Andrea, in more ways than one." As Andrea basked in his compliment, David turned to the Brooke, "And what do you do?"

Brooke had been distracted by whoops of laughter coming from the house. It sounded like the children were having a good time, anyway. David repeated the question, but Morgan answered for her.

"Brooke and I just relocated our family here from London where we spent the last three years. She's getting things under control on the home front while I swim with the sharks at the Phresh Music Group."

David mock bowed. "Welcome to New York—the media capital of the world."

Morgan tipped his glass towards David. "New York is great, but look behind you…Chicago and San Francisco are gaining on us."

David didn't hesitate. "I'm not complacent. I take my competitors very seriously. But here in the East we do have *The New Yorker*, *The Wall Street Journal*, and of course, *The New York Times*. Not to mention my own humble empire, *The New York Man*."

"No argument there, but…"

David interrupted, "GOM has been in the news a lot lately. You guys are giving Bertelsmann a run for their money."

Morgan was diplomatic. "We're trying. Tell me, David, what do you do at *The New York Man*?"

"I'm the Editor-in-Chief of the magazine. *New York Man's* parent company also owns a TV production company. We're piloting a new television series in the fall on NBC."

Wyatt looked interested. "I didn't know you were producing a TV show, David. I'm in negotiations with NBC for a new cooking show, myself. What's your show about?"

David sat forward in his chair. "Well, with the popularity of the *Queer Eye for the Straight Guy* we thought it would be fun to try *Gay Guy for the Cutie Pie.*"

Kathryn swiveled her head towards her ex. "Did I hear you correctly?"

David was unfazed. "My team finds girls with a lot of unrealized potential who are clueless about fashion, make-up, and style. Each week a new girl gets help from this really hip gay guy and his fashionista friends."

Kathryn gave him a withering look. "It sounds absolutely appalling."

Wyatt turned to James. "So James, what do you do for a living?"

"I'm a Wealth Manager."

Kathryn got up to help herself to a drink while James explained more about what he did.

"I was a Managing Director at Merrill for many years, but left last year to start my own company. We cater to high-net-worth individuals who, believe it or not, are relatively neglected. It's a niche we've been very successful in targeting."

Giselle asked, "Just how poor do these neglected millionaires have to be?"

"We're going after men, and women, who have portfolios of about $1 to $5 million in investable assets. Our research tells us that these are the customers who are becoming too small for the big boys like Goldman and Merrill."

Giselle shook her head back and forth. "Amazing."

Samantha asked James, "How did you meet Claire?"

"At the Bronxville library. My daughter, Alice, and I often go to the library on the weekends I have custody. Claire is working there part-time while she works on her Masters in Library Science. And of course, Alice knows Claire's son, Jake, since they were in the same fourth grade class last year."

Fumbling for words, Claire added, "Trip and I have been divorced for a number of years now, but we share custody of Jake, and James shares custody of Alice with Andrea. It's really working out great."

In the ensuing silence, Andrea just stared at the pool uncomfortably. She and James had a civil relationship for the sake of Alice, but socializing with him and his new girlfriend seemed a bit too much to ask.

Samantha gamely continued to try to spark a conversation. "So what do you do, Trip? How did you meet Kathryn?"

"We actually met in college, but we only recently started dating after we became reacquainted while chaperoning a fourth-grade class trip to the Metropolitan Museum. Our sons are the same age, and they get along great. The day after the class trip, I found a lame excuse to call Kathryn, something about clients of mine who needed some advice about a summer house, and luckily Kathryn didn't hang up on me. The rest, as they say, is history."

Kathryn smiled at Trip and stroked his arm. Something about the implied intimacy of their relationship rubbed David the wrong way.

"I'm sure everyone here agrees you two make a perfect couple, isn't that right Morgan?"

Before Morgan could respond, David continued, "In fact, they're so perfect that they've given me an idea for a new reality show. We could find old college sweethearts, reunite them, and then follow them on a few of their dates." David put his empty Margarita glass on the table and slowly rose to get another. He looked at the others and asked, "Wouldn't it be great to watch as the couples discover that their old flames are, well, old?"

Clearing his throat, Wyatt looked at Samantha and they both invited their guests to the dining tent to sample the buffet that was now set up. Their guests wholeheartedly welcomed the excuse to get up and focus on something they all could agree on—a fabulous meal.

Wyatt had outdone himself. Guests could choose from grilled sirloin, sliced off the bone, which had been lightly seasoned with rosemary; lobster rolls with fresh lobster meat, served on split, buttered and grilled brioche; charcoal-grilled shrimp; herbed-seasoned vegetables; and grilled stuffed mushrooms.

The children were also called and encouraged to sample the frankabobs and potatoes that Wyatt had created especially for the young palate. Pryce and Jake raced in first, well ahead of the girls. Hannah was happy to have two girls her age to play with so she wouldn't be stuck with her little sister Lily. While Lily and Jayne were busy giggling, Hannah was having more mature conversations with Alice and Charlotte. Their moms had already received the fifth grade class lists for the fall. Hannah and Alice were filling Charlotte in on the boys she would meet when school opened in the fall.

While the children raced through their meal so they could return to their indoor activities in the large, well-equipped basement, Samantha and Wyatt attempted to keep the conversation flowing while the adults finished their dinner. Andrea came to their rescue and asked Wyatt about how he got started as a personal chef.

Grateful for the diversion, Wyatt regaled the group with tales of some of the more famous clients he had cooked for when establishing his business in Westchester. His good friend Antony Ballard might boast that he was Chevy Chase's favorite chef, but Wyatt's clients were even more famous, and insisted he sign a nondisclosure statement that bound him to secrecy. He joked to his guests that if he disclosed the names of even one of his clients, he'd have to kill them. Kathryn volunteered that if Wyatt divulged the names to David, she'd be happy to let Wyatt kill him.

With a nervous laugh, Samantha rose and invited her guests outside for an after-dinner drink. As the adults ambled out of the dining tent toward the pool, Giselle touched Kathryn's arm. "I hope you don't mind, Kathryn, but the kids really wanted a Manny, so I hired Carlo for just a few afternoons a week. He's starting Monday."

Before Kathryn could utter a word, Giselle kicked off her Jimmy Choo's and walked toward the deep end of the pool. As the entire gathering watched, she pulled her shift over her head, and stepped onto the diving board in her hot pink bikini. If there had been any doubt before, Kathryn and everyone present now had visual confirmation of the rumors about Giselle's 40th birthday present to herself. They had all seen Giselle lounging at the club pool in previous summers, and she had never filled out a bikini top like that before.

Giselle dove into the pool and emerged at the shallow end. Shaking her wet blonde hair, she called, "Who wants to join me?"

As if Pavlov had rung a bell, every woman's arm shot out and automatically restrained her partner as he made a motion to rise. The only refreshing dip they were going to partake in was the leftover salsa from Wyatt's kitchen.

"If we had no winter, the spring would not be so pleasant; if we did not sometimes taste of adversity, prosperity would not be so welcome."

Anne Bradstreet

Chapter 6

The Gracious Garden

~~~

Not sure what to put in your terrace planters, which flowers and shrubs grow best in the shade, or how to update your garden with the newest varieties of perennials? Just ask local landscape architect, Chelsea Hollingsworth. One of the premier designers of gardens for homes and estate properties, Chelsea is a member of the Association of Professional Landscape Designers and the American Horticultural Society.

Minimum Bid: $500.

~~~

*B*rooke was looking forward to her consultation with Chelsea. Brooke really wanted to concentrate on the side yard and the area by the in-ground pool. Seated in the solarium, Brooke perused the tall pile of gardening magazines while she waited for Chelsea to arrive.

Mariella gently interrupted Brooke's reading to let her know that she had shown Chelsea into the living room. Brooke quietly thanked her and rose to welcome her guest.

Chelsea was standing by the window, admiring the silver-framed photographs on the Steinway piano. Brooke approached and offered her hand. "Chelsea, thank you so much for coming. I am so looking forward to hearing all of your ideas. Please, come and sit down on the sofa. Would you like some tea?"

Mariella entered the room with a silver tea service and set it on the low Hepplewhite table. Brooke offered to pour as Chelsea sank into the deep, plush cushion.

Chelsea made small talk asking about the various cities in which Brooke had lived and how often they had moved.

Brooke told her that while she enjoyed most of the places they had lived, it was time, if Chelsea would excuse the pun, *to put down roots.* "I can't wait to hear your suggestions for my backyard and get started creating something truly special."

Chelsea was happy to move the discussion to the real reason for her visit. While she had her own ideas about what might work best for Brooke and Morgan's property, she thought it important that Brooke articulate her own likes and dislikes. She began to probe about Brooke's preferences for color and types of foliage. Luckily Brooke seemed to have thought through many of the answers to Chelsea's questions.

Leaning forward in her chair, Chelsea began. "Please understand that there are no wrong answers to any of my questions. My goal is to create something that will exceed your expectations. But to do that, I need to know some basic things. For example, do you prefer a formal or informal feel?"

Brooke answered right away. "I would like it to be more informal. I really want this house to be a home. We've traveled so much and lived in so many places I couldn't call my own. I really want to make this a warm and inviting space."

"Is there a place or feeling you'd like to recreate? Do you want a place to remind you of summers spent at Martha's Vineyard, or was there a special garden in your childhood home or a friend's home that you visited?"

"I loved my Grandmother's estate in Philadelphia. When I was a little girl, I used to follow the family gardeners all over our property. They were very patient with me, and I almost believed I had a green thumb. As I got older, I dreamed of one day doing what you do. But deep down I knew I didn't have the passion and commitment for it that someone like you has."

Chelsea acknowledged Brooke's sentiment and encouraged her to continue.

"I still read tons of gardening magazines. And recently I took a two-hour flower arranging lesson with an event designer in San Francisco. It set Morgan back $1,000, but he didn't seem all that impressed with my creations. But I did learn something new. I now know the name of those disks with metal spikes that are placed at the bottom of a vase."

Chelsea laughed. "You mean the *frogs*. In the spring I use them all the time to anchor the stems of my tulips so that they remain in place and stand upright."

Brooke nodded. "When we were living in Asia, I heard it can take three to five years to master the techniques of ikebana, the ancient Japanese art of flower arrangement. We've never even been in one place for three to five years. I hope that pattern will be broken now that we've settled here."

Chelsea hoped so too. She asked, "How involved do you want to be in the project? We can make the decisions together as we go along, or you can tell me your vision and leave the rest up to me."

"I think it would be fun to participate in the decisions, but I am putting my total trust in you. I've already seen what you did over at Kathryn's house. It's magnificent."

Chelsea gracefully replied, "I really appreciate the kind words. I loved working on that property, but it was challenging. We did most of the major work while Kathryn and David were still married, and David didn't always share Kathryn's vision for the yard. But that's a moot point, now, since she got the house in the divorce settlement." Chelsea leaned in closer to Brooke. "But let's talk about you and your vision. You don't have to answer now, but there are things you need to think about before we move forward. For example, how will you use the space? Will your children use the backyard for recreation? Will you entertain outdoors a lot, or is it more of a private retreat? Will you use this space more during the day or night? What colors do you like? What colors do you dislike?"

Chelsea suggested they walk outside to get a better sense of the possibilities. Brooke readily agreed and led the way through the French doors to the terrace steps.

Heading through the arched gateway towards the pool area, Chelsea advocated for a romantic feel with roses such as "City Girl." This was one of her favorite varieties of climbers in pink and salmon shades that offered a profusion of double blooms in clusters. Moving well beyond the archway to the low stone walls that bordered the walkway to the pool, Chelsea suggested that they would look fabulous topped with "Beacon Silver."

The backyard presented wonderful opportunities to do something special. The first order of business was to choose a color theme. Brooke had recently had her colors done at a salon in Manhattan, and she didn't hesitate with a response. She told Chelsea she would love a pink and blue color theme that incorporated every imaginable hue—lavender, violet, mauve, magenta, salmon, dusty rose, and deep purple. Chelsea suggested Violet myrobalan as a focal point at the far end of the pool. Her mind was overflowing with ideas. "You could add in some Nymphenburg, Echinacea Purpurea, Oriental Poppy, and Phlox paniculata. And foliage in shades of dark green, blue green and blue gray would make a lovely accent." Chelsea's mind was racing with possibilities. "Along the stone steps leading to the pool, you could use violet blue spikes of veronica and coral pink echinacea. Or, if you preferred, white, lavender, mauve and dusty rose phlox would also work well." Chelsea turned back to face the terrace. "At the base of the steps leading from the terrace we could add benches, and cluster vibrant pink and white hydrangea. There are so many choices in this color scheme."

Chelsea reviewed the options for how the colors were arranged. She recommended putting the pastel shades further away, with bolder colors in the front. This would make the garden seem even larger than it was. Also, it was imperative that they mix perennials in the bed so that new colors would be blooming throughout the spring, summer and fall.

Next they talked about the area immediately surrounding the Olympic size swimming pool. Chelsea explained that plants and trees that hang over the pool might look magnificent, but they would be a major nuisance once the leaves and other plant material fell naturally into the pristine water. She cautioned Brooke to be sure that the flowers and shrubs were situated a good distance from the edge of the pool, not only for maintenance reasons, but also for the comfort of swimmers and guests lounging by the water. Groupings of earthenware pots containing vibrantly colored plants such as azaleas, tulips and cyclamens could be strategically placed along the perimeter to add some interest without creating havoc with pool maintenance."

Brooke was excited. She and Chelsea appeared to be on the same wavelength, and Brooke was able to visualize the ideas Chelsea had outlined. She couldn't wait to get started and asked Chelsea to write up a formal proposal on the spot. Chelsea sensed Brooke's genuine enthusiasm but cautioned her, "Beautiful gardens take time to develop."

Brooke didn't hesitate. "We plan on being here to see the garden develop."

It was only 11:30 and the kids were still in school, so Brooke invited Chelsea to stay for lunch. Chelsea didn't have any other consultations scheduled for the afternoon, so she gladly accepted. Brooke excused herself to go into the house to ask Mariella to prepare a light lunch and set it up on the patio.

Brooke quickly returned to the terrace, and she and Chelsea settled themselves into two of the comfy green lounge chairs to chat.

Chelsea initiated the conversation. "So how are you enjoying the Silent Auction items Morgan got for you?"

Brooke was momentarily at a loss for words as she remembered the Margarita Pool Party. "Jayne had the most wonderful time at her birthday party. And dinner at Sarah and Roger's was a lot of fun, wasn't it?"

Chelsea agreed. "Yes, dinner was delightful, and dessert at Giselle's was, shall we say, unusual? It certainly was a surprise seeing Giselle all dolled up in a French Maid's costume, but at least we weren't exposed to any kind of *wardrobe malfunction!*"

As Brooke's eyes widened, Chelsea asked her if she and Morgan had enjoyed the Margarita Pool Party.

Brooke hesitated, still unsure of how much to say. It had been a tense evening, and Giselle's skimpy bikini that left little to the imagination defied description.

Chelsea came to her rescue. "You don't have to say anything. Samantha and Wyatt are very good clients of mine. I heard the whole story from them…I'm just sorry I didn't bid on that auction item. I would love to have seen everyone's faces when Giselle acted like, well, Giselle. She's a bit over the top, but we love her anyway."

Brooke smiled. "Well, today was wonderful. I really can't wait to get started with the landscaping project."

Chelsea echoed the sentiments and added, "Kathryn told me you have a few more auction events coming up."

Brooke picked up her iced tea and took a sip. "We do have a few more things planned. I'm really looking forward to next month's excursion to Tiffany's, and the cruise in early December. Did I hear that you signed up for both of those events as well?"

Chelsea nodded her head. "Lizbet made sure I put my name on several of the bidding sheets."

Brooke was delighted. "Besides those events, Morgan and I are taking the kids skiing over Thanksgiving. We bid on Kathryn's condo in Vail."

"That should be nice. Just the family."

Brooke asked Chelsea about the last auction item, the Holiday House Tour.

Chelsea enthused, "That's always great fun. There will be a lot of people there, including yours truly. It's always a sell out. And since the Silent Auction events like that benefit our little red schoolhouse, I should probably ask you about how your kids are adjusting to it. Everything going okay with the teachers they got? Are they finding their way around the new building?"

"Jayne really loves second grade. It was a bit difficult for her at first, since this school keeps children in the same class for the first and second grade. The other kids were all used to the routine, the teacher, and each other, but she seems to have found her place. And Charlotte is happy to be in 5th grade. It's still such an innocent time, but I know those days are numbered."

Chelsea nodded vigorously. "It's true. It seems kids are taking an interest in dating, and the opposite sex, earlier and earlier. Wait until you see some of the outfits the girls try to wear in middle school. Keep your eyes open for some of the programs that are offered for parents to help us cope. Today's teens are going further—in more ways than one. I think if we knew everything that was really going on, we'd home-school our kids."

Brooke looked concerned. "But when and where are kids getting together?"

Chelsea ventured, "It could be at their own home while the parents are at work, or on the weekend when the parents are out, or at a friend's empty house. Don't be surprised when you hear about parents staying in the city overnight and trusting their teen to mind the manse. Believe me, having a teenager has curtailed our social life, such as it was. Ted and I won't go out unless someone is home. We're lucky, Ted's father is usually around, but if he's not, we just don't go out. The kids are too old for a babysitter, but not old enough to be left in the house unsupervised."

Brooke asked about drugs.

Chelsea frowned. "You may have heard about the high school boy who was arrested recently for giving drugs to a girl who ended up at Lawrence Hospital. Don't kid yourself. We are not immune here."

Brooke was concerned. "But what can we do?"

Chelsea was firm. "Just remember. Our kids have lots of friends. They don't need another friend, they need a parent."

Brooke was quiet for a few moments. "Well, I'm especially happy that Spencer and Michael have become friends. Dylan, too. Sarah and Roger should be proud of him—he's a really great kid. And it's reassuring to know that when my son is at your house or Sarah's house, he's in good hands."

Chelsea returned the compliment. "Thanks, I'm glad they're friends, too. Spencer will do fine. I know high school can be tough anywhere, but I think it's especially challenging in a place like Westchester. Did you ever hear about that memoir written by a young woman who grew up in Bronxville? Trust me, she didn't have too many fond memories of the Bronxville High School."

Brooke hadn't read the book.

Chelsea told her that the author of the "tell-all" had lived in a house not too unlike hers, but a few streets over. "I'd lend you my copy, but it might make you consider moving again!"

Brooke laughed out loud. "Oh, I'm sure it wouldn't do anything of the sort. How bad could it be?"

Chelsea just smiled in silence.

Brooke wasn't sure if Chelsea had been exaggerating, so she was happy when Chelsea changed the subject. "So what did Spencer do this summer?"

Brooke relaxed. "He went on one of those wilderness adventures in Jackson Hole. He loved it…backpacking and rock climbing the Teton Mountains; sea kayaking the waters of Yellowstone National Park and whitewater rafting through Snake River Canyon. How about your boys?"

"Ted and I wanted to take the whole family away for the month of August. We have a house on Martha's Vineyard, and Michael and Lucas hung out with their friends and us for a very relaxing vacation. It's rare that I can get Ted to take so much time away from his office, but with technology, he was able to keep things going from there for the month. I played on his guilt a little. I reminded him how it won't be long before the boys will be off vacationing without us."

Brooke was wistful. "Summer was great, but now we've all had to readjust to reality."

Chelsea agreed. "I'm the sure the kids will adjust quickly. Do they like walking to school?"

"Jayne and Charlotte love it. They just adore the crossing guard, Frank. He always has a kind word and a smile for them."

Chelsea agreed that he was special. "How about the homework? How has that been?"

Brooke groaned. "For Charlotte and Spencer, any homework is too much. High school is especially hard. I can't really help Spencer very much, especially with the math, and Morgan isn't home during the week all that much."

Chelsea commiserated. "Thank God for Ted's father. He was a math professor. I don't know what I'd do without him. He helps Michael and Lucas solve problems that I couldn't understand when I took math in school, and still can't figure out as an adult. What's more, I really don't see why we should care how fast Train A is going when it passes Train B, which is going 60 miles in the opposite direction. They'll both get to their destinations eventually."

Brooke was worried about the standardized tests. "What's all this talk about changes to the SAT now that our kids are getting closer to having to take the exam?"

Chelsea had heard some of the talk. "The SAT has always been criticized by those who say it favors students who can afford coaching. A lot of parents will tell you they oppose tutoring on principle, but when it comes to increasing their child's chances in the all important college admission game, well…"

Brooke was looking very concerned. "I've read that coaching is starting earlier than ever. Some think even Middle School is too late to start prepping."

Chelsea tried to reassure her. "Parents like Lizbet think Elementary School is too late!"

Brooke looked only slightly less concerned. "Maybe some good will come of the proposed changes. I hear that the math will be tougher, but they are doing away with those awful analogies."

Nodding her head, Chelsea added that "They're also adding some grammar, and most kids don't take grammar as a subject in high school. You've probably heard the horror stories of kids caught in that whole language movement who never learned grammar and spelling. I sound like my parents, but when I was a kid, we had to learn grammar and spelling by memory and repetition. Maybe Dick and Jane and Spot were ahead of their time."

Brooke asked Chelsea's advice about extra support. "I don't know what to do about a tutor. If I listen to Lizbet, I worry that Spencer will never get into any college because we haven't retained the tutor she used for Whitney in freshman year."

Chelsea tried to assuage her fears. "Keep in mind that there are those who think whether your child studies with an expensive private tutor or takes one of those Review courses, most of what the kids are learning is how to take a test."

Brooke sighed. "It's all very overwhelming. No wonder Lizbet has worked herself into a frenzy. I can see how this can really make any parent lose perspective."

Chelsea leaned forward. "I know you're neighbors, but let me give you a little piece of friendly advice. Lizbet is not any parent. If Whitney isn't inside the ivy-covered halls of Yale this time next year, you may want to consider moving, because there will be no living with that woman."

Brooke smiled and shook her head. "Oh, Chelsea, all the stories I've heard about Lizbet's obsession with getting Whitney into Yale can't possibly be true. I can't believe any parent would act that way, never mind one as smart as Lizbet."

Chelsea put down her glass of iced tea and looked directly at Brooke. "Brooke, a long time ago, my college roommate Shelby cut right to the heart of the matter when I had a hard time believing how some of our sorority sisters at Wellesley were behaving. Shelby had been studying about a very learned man named Julius Rosenwalk in her English Lit class. She was most impressed by his grasp of human nature, and I never forgot one of his most famous quotes.

Brooke listened attentively.

Chelsea raised her glass to Brooke and said, "Do not be fooled into believing that because a man is rich he is necessarily smart. There is ample proof to the contrary."

"So little time and so little to do."

Oscar Levant

Chapter 7

Breakfast at Tiffany's!

~ ~ ~

Dress to the nines for an elegant day in Manhattan. Join your hostess, Madison Winthrop, for a private tour of the world famous Tiffany vaults. Following your insider's look, let's do lunch at the incomparable La Grenouille and try on selected pieces from Madison's personal heirloom collection.

Of course, car service from Bronxville to Manhattan and back again will be provided!

Minimum Bid: $750

8 Highest bidders

~ ~ ~

*B*rooke dropped Jayne and Charlotte off at school and drove her silver Beemer to the hair salon at Neimman's. Geoffrey, the stylist who had been highly recommended by Lizbet, was already waiting for her.

"Geoffrey, make me look like Holly Golightly! I'm off to Tiffany's."

"Sweetheart, you are even more beautiful than Audrey Hepburn, but if it's what your heart desires, I'll give you a French twist that will make you look even more gorgeous than Audrey on her best day. Your brown hair is so silky soft that you make my job almost too easy."

Brooke relaxed and let Geoffrey work his magic. And magic it was. When she looked in the hand-held mirror so she could admire Geoffrey's handiwork, she couldn't help but smile. Her hairstyle was simple, but oh so elegant. With every hair in place, Brooke asked Marguerite to come over to apply her cosmetics while Celeste gave her a fresh manicure.

With time running out, Brooke headed over to the Designer Salon to meet her personal shopper Veronica and select a classic little black dress. The size 6 black crepe sheath that Veronica selected looked as if it would fit Brooke perfectly, but she wanted to try it on to be sure. As she opened the door to the dressing room, she saw that a body shaper, hose, and pair of black Peau de Soie pumps were already there.

Fully dressed, Brooke admired the total effect in the large mirrored dressing room and knew that Audrey herself would definitely approve. After charging her purchases and tipping her fairy godmothers for turning her into a princess, Brooke left Neimann's and headed home to await the limo. She knew there were seven other women besides the hostess, Madison, who would be together for the day. She had been introduced to Madison at the book club meeting Kathryn had invited her to, and they had both attended the dinner at Sarah and Roger's, but they hadn't had an opportunity to really get to know one another. Kathryn had only good things to say about Madison and how much she did for the School. Despite a demanding career as an investment banker, she was also a

School Board Trustee. It was awfully generous of Madison to take time out of her hectic day to host this always popular event.

Since Madison would be at her office in midtown, she would be meeting the group at Tiffany's main entrance. At precisely 11:00 the stretch limo pulled into Brooke's driveway. Brooke entered the car gracefully and said hello to everyone as they moved on to their last stop to pick up Lizbet and her close friend, Bitsy. Lizbet, the self-appointed leader of the group, ushered a petite blonde woman into the car and introduced her to the others.

"Everyone, I'd like you to meet one of my oldest and dearest friends, Bitsy Chandler." At Lizbet's urging, Bitsy sat forward and smiled at the others, revealing perfectly straightened and recently-whitened teeth. Bitsy crossed her legs, lady-like, as Lizbet gave the others a run down of their shared history.

"Bitsy and I pledged the same sorority and became the best of friends, more like sisters! We just know Whitney will be asked to join Kappa Alpha Theta once she gets her acceptance letter from Yale." As if on cue, Bitsy and Lizbet clasped hands and silently prayed to a higher power. Lizbet took a deep breath and continued. "Bitsy and her husband Elliot have just moved here from San Francisco. Brooke, you and Morgan lived there too, so you and Bitsy must have tons of friends in common." Brooke started to ask a question, but Lizbet wasn't finished. "Luckily for us, Elliot was transferred back east earlier this year. They bought that gorgeous old house on Prescott from that dreadful woman who tried to turn it into a McMansion. But that awful woman is not here now, and Bitsy is, so there you are!"

With a satisfied expression, Lizbet paused before telling Bitsy a little about each of the women already in the car.

"You already know Kathryn—the best real estate agent in Westchester County. Doesn't she know just about everyone and everything there is to know about Bronxville? I'll bet she knows when a divorce is on the horizon before half the husbands in town!"

Kathryn started to protest, but Lizbet dismissively waved away her protestations. "Right next to Kathryn is Brooke. She and her husband

Morgan just moved into the village with their three absolutely delightful children—Spencer, Charlotte and Jayne. Morgan has some big important job with that company that handles all those music artists we would never recognize, but our children know all about. Brooke doesn't know it yet, but she is going to chair a few of the events I'm planning for the spring. I am going to be keeping her very, very busy!"

Before Brooke could respond, Lizbet hastened to introduce the others in the limo.

"And this is Sarah. Sarah is newly "retired" from J. P. Morgan Chase Bank One or whatever her former employer is called these days. Her talented daughter Ruthann is at Georgetown, and her handsome son Dylan is in the high school. I'll bet Sarah would love to join our bridge club, and the garden club, and maybe the hospitality committee for the high school. We could certainly put her talents to good use, couldn't we Bitsy? We are just going to have to plan a lot of activities for Sarah now to fill her days, won't we?"

Lizbet turned slightly. "Don't you hide in the corner there, Chelsea Hollingsworth. Chelsea is *the* landscaper for you when you finish restoring your house. We just have to make sure that Chelsea can fit you into her schedule! Chelsea is almost as busy as I am! Besides her own landscaping business, she consults with the New York City Beautification Council, and heads up the Bronxville Arbor Society. What a dynamo."

Before Chelsea could utter a word, Lizbet pointed to Giselle. "And that tall blonde whose legs are taking up all the room in this limo is Giselle Ceravalo. In case you couldn't tell, Giselle was a model. Of course she still could be a model, but now she has turned her talents to designing lingerie. You should see the line of classic peignoirs she made for me in every color imaginable. I especially love the new seashell pink one. Pink, as you all know, is the new black." Lizbet turned to her friend. "I'm sure Giselle would be delighted to design some just for you, too, Bitsy."

Carole cringed as she realized she was the next target of Lizbet's monologue. "This is Andrew Grayson's wife, Carole. She and Andrew live over on Sagamore in one of those cute little walk-up apartments. It's just darling."

Carole slunk back in the seat as Lizbet forged ahead. "But I have to warn you, Bitsy, you'd better hold onto your Gucci wallet. Carole is always busy raising funds for some wonderful organization or another, and I'm sure she'll be inviting you and Elliot to scads of exciting events!"

Bitsy thanked everyone for making her feel welcome and told them how much she was looking forward to their tour and lunch. While the chauffeur took the FDR Drive to get them to 5th Avenue and 57th Street, Lizbet settled back into the leather seat and asked who in the group knew the history of Tiffany's. Without waiting for a response, she launched into an impressive review of the facts. She had obviously done her homework. She told the ladies how on September18, 1837, Charles Lewis Tiffany and John B. Young established Tiffany & Young, a stationery and fancy goods emporium on Broadway in New York City. Their first day's sales total of $4.98 wouldn't even pay for fifteen minutes in the parking garage today.

Lizbet went on to tell everyone all about when the famous Tiffany blue box was introduced, when the first Blue Book catalog was published, and when the "Tiffany Setting," a six-prong diamond solitaire engagement ring, made its debut.

As they turned onto 57th Street, she looked at each of the ladies and asked, "Who knows which mythical bronze figure presides over the main entrance of Tiffany's?"

Lizbet caught Bitsy's eye and they both shouted "Atlas" at the same time. Brooke was getting the distinct feeling that these two were inseparable.

The limo driver made a smooth stop right at the front entrance of Tiffany's. As the driver helped each of the women alight from the car, Madison came through the front door of the store and made her way over to greet the group. Lizbet instructed the driver to be sure to be in that exact spot to pick them up in an hour.

Satisfied that they were all ready, the ladies approached the entrance where an armed guard met them as they passed beneath the statue of Atlas and entered the famed landmark. The guard led them to a spacious wood-paneled elevator in the back of the building and escorted them to their destination on the third floor. In a hushed private room, Madison invited the group to sample a light "breakfast" served on the traditional Tiffany bone china with sterling silver flatware, in the classic shell and thread motif, while they awaited the arrival of Genevieve.

The ladies selected from a wide variety of specialty teas and assorted pastries and made quiet conversation. Gracefully holding her platinum-edged china teacup and speaking with Carole, Brooke almost didn't hear the door behind her open. Two large men and an impeccably dressed woman entered the room. The men deposited three large cases on a sideboard and placed large rectangular velvet display pads on the mahogany table.

Madison rose to greet the newcomers. As the women sipped their tea, Madison introduced Genevieve, their Tiffany guide, who artfully arranged the exquisite pieces from the first case on the table. Genevieve invited the ladies to feel free to touch each piece and hold it up for closer examination.

After a time, they group settled back in their chairs as Gen described some of the more popular pieces. "I see that several of you admired the Lily of the Valley brooch with 63 amethysts set in platinum. The 18K gold leaves on the pin are set with 50 round tsavorites and 31 Tiffany diamonds."

There were several oohs and aahs as Gen continued. "And those rare blue-diamond drop earrings are truly exceptional. To match two such diamonds was an incredible feat."

Kathryn asked the price of the pink tourmaline ring she had her eye on. Gen told her it retailed for $31,000. Without consulting any notes, she told Kathryn that the stone was 7.38 carats, extraordinarily bright, deep and even, and surrounded by 58 Tiffany diamonds.

Bitsy couldn't wait to hear about the next piece—a Diamond Art Deco style bracelet. Gen explained that it would sell for $82,000. It had an astonishing 395 Tiffany diamonds, for a total weight of 16.63 carats.

While Bitsy kept all her attention on the bracelet, Brooke wanted to know about that aquamarine and diamond pendant that Gen had picked up. Gen explained, "It's a bit less…only $27,150. It has 18 round aquamarines and 107 round brilliant Tiffany diamonds."

After a final look at the magnificent pieces, Genevieve restored the jewelry to their original cases. The guards carried the cases back to the vault while Gen chatted with the ladies and answered their remaining questions. When the men returned, they were carrying shopping bags with long blue Tiffany boxes fastened with white silk ribbons. Madison had very thoughtfully arranged for each of the women to receive a Tiffany cashmere scarf as a memento of the visit.

As it was getting late, Madison thanked the Tiffany staff and guided her friends downstairs to prepare for lunch. The ladies re-entered their limo, which was dutifully waiting in the designated spot, to make the short drive over to East 52nd Street between 5th and Madison. The owner of La Grenouille, the famous midtown restaurant known for its perfect haute cuisine, was expecting them.

The maitre'd warmly welcomed Madison, whom he appeared to know quite well, and escorted the ladies to the private room upstairs. Brooke loved the stunning effect of the two-tiered dining room with leaded glass windows, French doors with Juliet balcony, and wood-burning fireplace.

Madison often entertained clients at La Grenouille, and the staff always took special care to ensure that her events were flawlessly planned and executed. Already waiting at each place setting was an engraved lunch menu selected by Madison's administrative assistant in consultation with the Head Chef. A Tiffany note card with each woman's name in calligraphy indicated where each woman should take her seat.

The tuxedoed waiters held out the chairs for the ladies and ensured they were all comfortable before requesting their drink order.

Amuse-Bouches
Canapes

Potage de Potiron
Butternut Squash Soup,
Pumpkin Oil and Seeds

Filet de Saumon Grille
Forestiere, Beurre
Nantais
Grilled Salmon
Forestiere, Lemon butter
Sauce

Napoleon aux
Framboises, Glace a la
Cannelle
Raspberry Napoleon,
Cinnamon Ice Cream

Petits Fours
Et Truffes au Chocolat
After Luncheon Sweets
and Chocolate Truffles.

After everyone made their lunch selections, Madison asked the group if they would like to look at a few of her favorite pieces that had been in her family for generations. One of the Tiffany security guards who had joined them at the restaurant appeared at her side. He unlocked an attaché case and carefully set the pieces on taupe velvet pads. Madison had brought only four pieces that she thought the women would especially like. Most were passed down to her from her grandmother, who collected jewelry from the Art Deco period.

The first piece was an antique platinum diamond and sapphire brooch that was made in 1915. The diamonds were all graduated, clear white, and European cut. At the center of the brooch was a large 3-carat diamond. Brooke sighed. Her grandmother had a brooch just like it, but Brooke didn't know what had happened to it after her grandmother passed away. While she thought the piece was quite beautiful, Brooke was more interested in it because of its sentimental value.

The second piece was an exquisite Tiffany Art Deco Bow Brooch, full of color and movement. The piece was pave-set with diamonds, and beautifully accented by onyx "ribbons" and emerald and ruby flowers. Brooke held the brooch up to her black dress and asked Giselle how it looked. Giselle didn't hesitate. "Stunning, absolutely stunning. By the way, did anyone ever tell you look like Audrey Hepburn?"

Brooke blushed. "Actually, Morgan told me that the night we met."

The guard walked around the table with the two rings Madison had selected to share. The first was an emerald-cut sapphire, diamond and platinum ring. The other was her grandmother's engagement ring, a classic six-prong, diamond solitaire Tiffany engagement ring.

The dazzling pieces seemed to take everyone's breath away and the room was unnaturally quiet. Lizbet seized the opportunity to take control of the conversation. "Madison, these pieces are simply exquisite. I, for one, hope that someday my Whitney gets an engagement ring as beautiful as the one you just showed us…maybe the stone could be just a little bigger, though, to show off Whitney's long, slender fingers. She has my fingers, you know."

Bitsy nodded in agreement as Lizbet continued, "Anyway, you are all too quiet. You must be thinking some very interesting thoughts. Kathryn?"

Kathryn held up the Tiffany engagement ring the guard handed her. "Actually, I'm remembering when David surprised me with a trip to Paris and proposed over dinner at L'Orangerie. On bended knee, he presented me with a 3-carat Tiffany diamond ring. That seems like a lifetime ago."

Brooke went next. "I was just thinking about taking my grandmother's jewelry out of the safe and wearing it more often. What's the sense in having such beautiful things if you can't enjoy them?"

Lizbet agreed. "Bitsy, how about you? What's going through your mind?"

"I was just trying to figure out how to convince Elliot to get me that diamond bracelet Genevieve showed us earlier. We do have an anniversary coming up."

Lizbet assured her they would come up with a plan together. She turned to Sarah. "Sarah? What do you think about the pieces we've seen?"

"Actually I wasn't thinking about jewelry at all. I was thinking that even though I love being back in Manhattan, I am so happy I don't have to go back to work after our lunch. My old office was just a few blocks over on Lexington Avenue."

Lizbet turned to Chelsea and asked what was on her mind.

"I was just thinking I'd need a whole new wardrobe to go with the jewelry, unless they came out with the Tiffany Jeans and cotton tees collection."

Giselle nudged Chelsea. "Why don't you try dressing up once in a while? You just might like it." Chelsea raised her eyebrows as if highly insulted. After a pregnant pause, she burst out laughing, and everyone relaxed.

Lizbet moved on to Carole. "How about you?"

Carole was actually thinking that if she wanted to write off most of the $750 she had to bid for this event, she'd better talk business. "I was just reflecting on how generous it was of Madison to arrange all this. She did such a beautiful job—not that any of us are surprised. I'm just hoping that in the spring Madison and John will co-chair a charity fundraiser for the

Youth Arts Council. I know that with Madison involved, it would be a huge success."

The group politely applauded for Madison as Lizbet asked her, "Penny for your thoughts?"

Madison wasn't going to give her thoughts for a penny—especially since they were not very charitable. She wondered for the umpteenth time how Lizbet had bamboozled her into agreeing to host this event. She was so busy at work, and she'd pay in more ways than one for this extended lunch. She had a Working Women of Bronxville meeting this evening which she did not want to miss, and she wasn't sure how she'd finish everything she had to do so she could catch the 7:05 out of Grand Central. Smoothly sidestepping Lizbet's query, Madison discretely signaled the waiter.

"Excuse me, ladies, but I see that our first course is ready. *Bon Appétit!*"

"To succeed in the world it is not enough to be stupid, you must also be well-mannered."

Voltaire

Chapter 8

A Cozy Chalet

~~~

"Spend a glorious week in a secluded retreat nestled in the Aspen Trees of West Vail. The recently refurbished home includes two master bedrooms, three additional bedrooms, five baths and a gourmet kitchen. There's an additional loft/entertainment room, and a large deck with hot tub to enjoy the breathtaking views. Located just a short distance from Vail village, Lionshead and the Cascade Club, you'll find everything you need for a spectacular getaway vacation.

No smoking, no pets, and no unaccompanied children, please."

Minimum Bid: $3,000

~~~

*K*athryn was relieved that Morgan had been the successful bidder for her Vail condo. This was the fifth year she had offered the use of the condo as a Silent Auction item, and the winners weren't always people she would necessarily have chosen to stay at her home. Even though she always clearly specified no smoking and no pets, she knew her request wasn't always followed. Even more frustrating was when a family that won kept changing the date they wanted to reserve. But with Brooke and Morgan, Kathryn didn't even mind that they wanted a prime week in November when so many families from the East Coast would be descending on the ski resort for a long weekend of Thanksgiving skiing. She and Trip already had plans to go to London to visit with friends for the holiday.

Kathryn loved her condo *and* loved the fact that David had wanted it desperately, but had lost that battle in the divorce settlement. He certainly was not accustomed to being told "No" to anything he wanted. While they were married, he had always liked to go skiing over Thanksgiving. Kathryn hoped he and his new girlfriend would have to find some outrageously priced hotel that wasn't nearly as convenient to the slopes.

Before the Braithwaites left for the airport, Kathryn made sure Brooke had her cell phone number and told her to call her if there was anything at all that she needed to make it a terrific vacation. On the morning of their flight, the Braithwaites arrived at LaGuardia Airport in two cars, since they could not fit the family and all of their luggage in one sedan. The driver of the first taxi led the way to the American terminal and pulled up curbside. Morgan overtipped the drivers as they handed over the mountains of luggage to a skycap. With only their small carry-on bags, the family headed for the Admirals Club to wait for their flight. Once inside the hushed haven, the kids spread out and settled into comfy chairs. Spence pulled out his iPod; Charlotte turned on *Eloise at the Plaza* on her DVD player; and Jayne extracted her cobalt Advanced Gameboy from her overstuffed backpack. Morgan selected a seat at a large square table and set up his laptop to check his e-mail while sipping a Perrier. Brooke offered to get the kids warm chocolate chip cookies and juice. At Morgan's prodding, Spencer got up to help his mother and grabbed a Sprite for himself.

In what seemed like no time at all, early boarding was called and the family gathered their gear and headed for the gate. After showing their passports and boarding documents, Morgan led the family through the curtain to first class. He and Brooke took the first two seats. Behind them, Jayne and Charlotte settled in, while Spencer happily occupied his own row. Brooke reminisced with Morgan about the long-haul flights they used to take from London to Bahrain, and then on to Sydney, on Gulf Air. The only saving grace was that the airline offered Sky Nannies trained by Norland College in England that helped with boarding and meals, and kept the kids entertained. Hopefully all the electronics the kids had brought with them on this vacation would keep them occupied during the relatively short flight.

The flight attendant offered champagne or mineral water. Morgan accepted the champagne while Brooke chose the water. The kids were not interested in another drink. Charlotte was too busy showing Jayne how to operate the personal video system for her seat.

Once the airplane reached cruising altitude, Morgan stood up to use the restroom. On his way back, he stopped to see how Spencer was doing.

At his Dad's tap on the shoulder, Spencer took off his earphones and looked up. "Whassup?"

Morgan asked if he needed anything before he returned to his seat.

Spencer didn't hesitate. "A black sapphire metallic BMW Z4."

Morgan ruffled Spencer's hair and turned back to his seat.

"Wait. Dad, how are we getting to the condo once we land?"

Morgan leaned on Spencer's seat. "We're renting an SUV at the Denver airport. We'll make better time driving the rest of the way than waiting for the connecting flight to Vail."

Spencer perked up. "Can I drive the car from the airport to the condo?"

Morgan laughed. "I know we've been out of the States for some time, but I wasn't aware that the Department of Motor Vehicles was now issuing learner's permits to 15 year olds."

"C'mon, Dad. How am I ever going to learn to drive if I don't practice? All my friends' parents let them practice."

"When you're 16, you can practice all you want. Assuming, that is, that your grades are up to par."

Spencer rolled his eyes and put his earphones back on so he could resume listening to *Outkast*.

Charlotte was eavesdropping and took immense delight in the fact that Spencer couldn't drive yet. He missed no opportunity to remind her how much older he was and how much more he was able to do. Even getting ready for this trip, he had reminded her that he had skied in the European Alps, but she had been too young. The family skied often, but surprisingly, none of them had ever been to Vail.

Brooke stood up to check on the girls. Charlotte asked her mother what Colorado was going to be like. Brooke repeated some of the things Kathryn had told her when giving her the keys and directions to the condo. Brooke reached into her Prada tote and pulled out the brochure Kathryn had given her. "Well, honey, it says here that Vail is North America's number one ski resort. Vail Village and Lionshead form the heart of the quaint Town of Vail."

Brooke handed Charlotte the brochure. "Look at this picture. It looks so peaceful, doesn't it? See the clock towers at the base of the slopes. It's very picturesque, don't you think?"

Charlotte nodded and asked, "How far away is the place we'll be staying?"

"The house is on the slopeside path of a place called Beaver Dam. It should be really convenient. Ms. Chasen says there is ski-in, ski-out access right from her back door."

Charlotte squirmed in her seat. "I want to ski every day!"

"You will honey. We've hired ski nannies for you and Jayne."

Morgan, who'd been only half listening, raised his eyebrows. As Brooke sat back down, he said in a low voice, "What the hell is a ski nanny?"

Brooke explained. "The ski nannies will come to the house in the morning, pick up Jayne and Charlotte, and take them directly to their ski lessons. After the lessons, they'll pick them up and bring them back to wherever we tell them we'll be. Spence will be fine on his own. We'll just have to be sure he brings his cell phone for emergencies." Brooke touched Morgan's arm. "Speaking of cell phones, promise me you'll use your cell phone only to communicate with us, not GOM."

Morgan looked his wife in the eye. "Brooke, when I'm skiing, the last thing I want is to have my phone vibrating while I'm up on the chair or taking off on a run."

Brooke rummaged in her bag to double check that she had brought enough cell phones for the family. She pulled out the small silver and pink one she would give to Jayne when they arrived. "I just hope the reception is good in case the kids need to get in touch with us."

Morgan wasn't optimistic about the reception. "A guy who works for me says that Sprint has the best service at Vail. Not surprisingly, an executive from Sprint owns a house on the mountain. Since we have Verizon, it would have been nice if their top guy had a house there, too."

Brooke put Jayne's phone back in her bag and relaxed in her seat. "I'm really looking forward to this uninterrupted family time without the distractions of your job, our friends, video games, school work, sports, and the millions of other things that make up our daily lives. I want to ski, but I'm also looking forward to exploring the restaurants, shops, and galleries while you're skiing. Morgan, I hope you can relax."

Morgan reassured her. "When I'm on the slopes, all I'm thinking about is my next turn. With my knees, I need to stay focused and stay vertical. It's such an awesome feeling when you find your rhythm and move with the terrain…and this time I'll be trying out the new Fusion skis I bought."

"They look really nice, Morgan. I'm sure you'll love them."

"Look nice, yeah, but I'm more impressed that they figured out how to put the binding interface in the body of the ski instead of on top of it. It's supposed to be much more flexible and make for easier turns."

Brooke thumbed through the latest copy of *Ski Magazine* the flight attendant had offered. "Well, I'm looking forward to trying out the new gloves I bought for all of us. Supposedly you just blow into the tiny hole in each glove and the warm air circulates to your fingertips, keeping your hands nice and toasty."

"You should have saved your money. What did they set us back, about $100 a pop?"

Brooke looked offended. "They were a little more than that, but they're worth it. I hate being cold, and these sounded ideal. Don't you think they'll work?"

Morgan laughed. "Oh, I'm sure they'll work fine, but that assumes the kids don't lose them by the first day. Maybe this time one will lose the right glove and the other, the left, so we'll still have one complete set."

Brooke made a face at him and changed the subject. "What's this new thing Spence is talking about doing—free something?"

Morgan explained. "It's called free-riding. He wants to go to some kind of new terrain park that sounds like a mother's worst nightmare. Adventure Ridge is a recreation park where they have evening snowboard-ing, freeskiing, ice skating, ski bikes, and laser tag." Morgan gestured with his hands as he described how the snow was shaped over ramps that sent the skiers into the air. "They have all the things you feared when he had his skateboard—half-pipes, long U-shaped chutes, and hairpin turns."

Brooke frowned. "Why don't we stick to something the whole family can enjoy, like tubing? There's no special skill required, and every member of our family can manage to slide down the mountain in a giant inflated tube."

Morgan advised her not to worry about Spencer. Instead, he wanted her to fill him in on all the details Kathryn had given her. Brooke informed him that Kathryn's condo had not only all the basics—two master suites, several guest rooms, a fully-equipped kitchen, washer/dryer, cable TV, stereo—but also a lot of terrific extras, including two Jacuzzi tubs, multiple fireplaces, and breathtaking 360 degree mountain views.

Morgan was looking forward to all of it, especially the Jacuzzi that would help him relax after the flight. "It sounds great. I know you said that there's a kitchen, but how much are you planning to cook? What do you want to do about Thanksgiving dinner?"

Brooke shrugged her shoulders. "I'm sure we'll find a nice restaurant."

A small voice from behind them asked, "McDonalds?"

Brooke turned around. "No, Jayne, some place that will have turkey and all the trimmings."

Morgan asked about the idiosyncrasies of the condo. "Did you speak with Kathryn to be sure we know about any quirks of the house…locks that have to be jiggled, how to turn on the heat, and whatever else we might need to know?"

"Yes. Kathryn assured me there shouldn't be any problems. She told me we should park in the two-car garage and then go through the door in the garage that leads into a mud room. If we continue through the downstairs den and guest bedrooms, we'll come to a heated paved patio with a sunken hot tub." Morgan thought it sounded perfect.

Brooke described the rest of the house. "Upstairs on the main level, there should be a great room with cathedral ceilings and huge windows so we can really enjoy the views, which she tells me are spectacular. There will be a large rock fireplace off the kitchen and breakfast bar. From the main level, we can head up a staircase to the two master bedroom suites and two additional guestrooms."

Before Morgan could ask any more questions, the flight attendant began preparations for landing and reminded them to turn off all electronic equipment. Brooke got Spencer's attention and he removed his earphones just as the Captain came on the loudspeaker to thank them for flying with American and wish them a pleasant stay in Colorado.

Disembarking was smooth, and the Braithwaites took the escalator down to the baggage area. As their luggage was first off the aircraft, Morgan and

Spencer quickly retrieved their suitcases and equipment from the slow-moving carousel without too much trouble. Morgan hailed a porter, and the family made a bee-line for the rental counter. The paperwork was in order, so they headed towards the garage to pick up their assigned Lexus SUV.

Snow was falling at a steady pace as they drove up the ramp and out of the airport garage. Jaynie opened the window, and stuck her tongue out to catch the falling snowflakes. Once on the road, they tuned in to the local weather report and cheered when they heard that record snowfall was expected over the next few days. With the weather report confirmed, Spencer was given the nod that it was okay to fiddle with the radio to find a "good" station.

Brooke pulled out the map the rental clerk had given them and read off the detailed directions. The girls were antsy, but she assured them they would be at the house within an hour. They would get some dinner, unpack, and get to bed early so that they were ready to hit the slopes first thing in the morning. The girls soon nodded off, Spencer listened to his music, and Morgan and Brooke spent the rest of the ride in companionable silence. Brooke pulled out her Super Flight Cream and rubbed it all over her hands to counter the harsh effects of the high altitude. She also applied a fresh coat of Jurlique Lip Care Balm to protect her lips from the freezing temperatures.

It wasn't too long before Morgan passed through Vail Village and approached the last turn that would take them to Kathryn's house. He saw a huge house up on the right and guided the car around the mounds of freshly plowed snow to her driveway.

As soon as he turned off the car, the kids scrambled out. He told them it was okay to leave the luggage in the car while they explored the house. When they returned from dinner later he'd pull the car into the garage to make it easier to unload.

The house, the mountain, the snow, the moonlight…everything was so peaceful and beautiful. They could glimpse a part of the back deck that led right out onto the mountain, just as Kathryn had told them. As they huddled around the main entrance to the house, Brooke found the key and opened the front door.

Morgan led the way through the downstairs den so he could check out the covered patio and hot tub. He was tired from traveling and couldn't wait to soak away his fatigue. He turned the handle on the sliding door to the outside deck.

Looking back on it later, Morgan wasn't sure who was more surprised at that moment. As soon as he stepped out into the moonlight, he heard David and Andrea laughing as they sipped champagne in the hot tub. At his approach, Andrea dropped her glass on the deck where it landed with a thud.

David looked unruffled. "Morgan! What a nice surprise! I believe you've met my friend, Andrea. I think it was at Wyatt and Samantha's pool party. I'd get up, but..."

Morgan commanded, "Don't get up!" He was not amused. Through clenched teeth, Morgan slowly asked David, "What are you doing here?"

David waved his glass as he spoke. "I knew Kathryn was in London—with Pryce—to visit her friend Cynthia for the holiday. She didn't mention that she had offered the condo to anyone...I still have a key I forgot to return, and so I just thought..."

Morgan seethed. "Get out."

"No need to raise our voices. It's just a small snafu. Why don't we just have a drink..."

Morgan stepped closer and raised his voice an octave. "Perhaps the altitude has affected your hearing, so let me be perfectly clear." He drew out each word menacingly. "Find...other...accommodations."

"But, Morgan, old man, there is nothing available. It's Thanksgiving week, and everything's been booked for months. Why don't we just have a nice glass of champagne and work this out like gentlemen."

Morgan smiled and David relaxed back into the hot tub. "You're right, David, I am a gentleman. Andrea, you are welcome to stay in one of the guestrooms down here. David, my wife and I are going to the restaurant for dinner with our children. By the time we return, I expect that you will have found alternative accommodations. Should you choose not to vacate the premises, I guarantee you will not be pleased with the alternative I choose for you."

Morgan turned towards his family who stood transfixed behind the open glass door. "Brooke, kids, let's go get some dinner. I saw a terrific restaurant on Gore Creek Road that I think we should try while our 'guest' gathers his belongings."

Before heading back through the sliding door, Morgan looked down at David. "Cheer up, *old man*. If you can't find another place to stay, I'd be happy to call Kathryn. I'm sure she would be delighted to introduce you to the local law enforcement personnel. I'm sure they could find you accommodations for the night."

David scowled while Andrea sunk even lower in the hot tub.

As the Braithwaites departed, Jayne removed her hand from her mother's and ran back to the deck. Before her parents could stop her, they heard her small voice wishing David and Andrea a "Happy Thanksgiving."

Brooke tilted her head as she looked up at Morgan expectantly. She reminded him of one of his mother's favorite sayings "to strive to be the person your dog thinks you are."

After a long silence, Morgan's shoulders sagged in defeat.

"Alright, alright. The turkey can stay."

"Hard work never killed anybody, but why take a chance."

Edgar Bergen

Chapter 9

Sailing Away

~~~

Need some pampering?

Grab your best girlfriend—or better yet—all your best girlfriends and sail away on a 4 day/3 night cruise aboard the luxurious Star Princess. Each day you can choose to participate in fitness classes or select from an unbelievable array of pampering treatments—facial and nail therapies; massages and bodywork; spa hand and foot treatments exfoliation; body wraps; hydrotherapies, and more. Enjoy gourmet meals and deluxe accommodations that will take you to a place where your everyday routines are just a memory.

Winning bidders will also receive a spa outfit designed by our very own designer, Giselle Ceravalo.

Minimum Bid: $2,000 - all inclusive

~~~

*T*he sleek black town car arrived at Brooke's door promptly at 11:00 a.m. on Friday. Brooke had already said her goodbyes to the children since she wouldn't be home until Monday afternoon. Their nanny had agreed to stay through the weekend, and her housekeeper Mariella would be around, so Brooke could leave without any worries on the home front.

Eight women had successfully bid on this cruise, so Brooke would have lots of company. Three were already in the limo—Lizbet, Madison, Sarah; the others—Chelsea, Kathryn, Carole and Giselle—would take a separate car and meet them at the pier in Manhattan. They were all sorry that Francesca couldn't take Friday and Monday off from school. Bitsy had also wanted to come, but Lizbet had told them that Bitsy was attending her husband's law school reunion at Stanford this weekend. (Boring!)

The driver took the Cross County Parkway to the Henry Hudson and quickly delivered them to the Princess Cruise line's terminal at 52nd Street in Manhattan. The porters stationed by the curb quickly and efficiently took charge of the various sets of matched luggage.

Lizbet had already given each of them a brochure from *Gramatan Travel* with all the details about the cruise, so they had a pretty good idea what to expect. This was a luxury cruise to nowhere. They would sail out into the Atlantic Ocean and just relax at sea for the next few days. Judging by the itinerary outlined in the brochure, there would be plenty to do on their floating luxury hotel over the next few days.

Brooke and Lizbet chatted amiably as they entered the terminal and headed towards the Information Desk to meet the others. Madison was checking her Blackberry one last time, and Sarah was on her cellphone. Lizbet immediately spotted Giselle and Chelsea and waved to get their attention. Carole and Kathryn were just coming out of the Ladies Room. After much excited hugging and air kisses, all the women approached the Princess Cruise Line check-in staff to present their passports and get their cruise cards.

Since everything was in order, the group proceeded up the gangway and stepped onto the Star Princess. A handsome officer in dress whites welcomed the women aboard. He pointed them in the direction of their rooms and wished them a pleasant cruise.

Brooke and Kathryn were sharing a cabin on the Royal Promenade Deck. In the room next to them were Lizbet and Giselle. The others had cabins on the Verandah Deck; Madison and Sarah were sharing one room; in the other, Chelsea and Carole had paired up.

Lizbet had requested that everyone settle in and then meet in the Serenity Seas Café for the buffet lunch before they set sail. She took Giselle by the arm and hurried her off to find their accommodations.

Kathryn found her cabin easily and unlocked the door for herself and Brooke. As they stepped inside, the cabin steward knocked softly on the open door to introduce himself and tell them to let him know if they needed anything at all. Kathryn told him the luggage could wait, but she just noticed some champagne on the table that looked like it needed to be opened immediately. He bowed and silently stepped over to the side table that held a silver ice bucket with a bottle of Moet & Chandon. Next to the bucket was an oval tray with a mouthwatering array of red, ripe strawberries dipped in rich, dark chocolate. Brooke and Kathryn toasted Lizbet's attention to detail. The cruise was definitely off to a promising start.

Brooke was looking forward to sailing away, but she missed the bon voyage parties she remembered attending as a child. But with all the new security regulations, no one was allowed on board unless they were passengers. At least they had each other to throw confetti on and stand beside as they watched the incomparable New York skyline recede.

* * *

Carole and Chelsea were the last ones to get to the Serenity Seas Café and join their friends at a long table by a bank of windows. Over a light lunch of salad, fruit and yogurt, the ladies discussed what they wanted to do for the afternoon as they looked out at the Atlantic Ocean.

Lizbet reminded the group, "Don't forget to sign up for the yoga and fitness classes in the Ship Shape Salon on Deck 10 Forward, and then take the spa tour on Deck 11 Aft. At the end of the tour, you can sign up for your facial, massage, nail and hair appointments for the next few days. There are 25 massage, body and skin care treatment rooms, and I intend to see them all!"

Chelsea interjected, "But I wanted to sit by the pool this afternoon."

Lizbet flipped her hair away from her face with her bejeweled right hand. "Fine, but don't complain when all the best appointments are taken and you leave the cruise looking as harried as you do now."

Several voices shouted, "Lizbet!"

"I'm sorry, I'm just trying to be helpful, you know."

Carole spoke up. "Chelsea, you sit by the pool. I'll schedule your appointments for you. I'm going there anyway."

Lizbet continued. "And don't forget the emergency drill at 4:00. Make sure you put on those darling orange vests at proceed to your Muster station."

Carole looked confused. "Our what?"

Giselle was horrified. "Orange?"

Lizbet looked smug. "Muster station. That's where you meet for the emergency drill, and you must wear your life vest. So try to wear something that goes with orange so you don't look as ridiculous as the other passengers. Orange just does not go well with my complexion but I always make the best of it by changing my lipstick so it doesn't clash."

Madison rolled her eyes while Chelsea stifled a laugh.

Oblivious to the reactions, Lizbet moved on to review the evening activities. "I made all the arrangements for dinner in the Grand Ballroom. We have the 8:30 seating so we won't be bothered by any small children. I love children, of course, but this cruise is just for us. We really need to relax."

Lizbet consulted her list of notes and proceeded with the agenda. "After dinner we're going to the *Best of Broadway* show in the Atlantis Theatre, and then we'll have drinks in the Schooner Bar."

She smiled brightly, revealing her perfectly whitened teeth. "Any questions?

Carole muttered under her breath. "When are we scheduled to go to the bathroom?"

Lizbet brightened. "Did someone ask about the bathrooms? Yes, the bathrooms in the cabins are just a wee bit small, but you won't be spending any time in your rooms. Ladies, we are going to have so much fun!"

One by one the women rose to find their way to their activities. By the time the afternoon and evening program Lizbet had planned was over, everyone was tired and ready to return to their cabins. The cabin steward had refreshed their towels, turned down the beds, and left a rich chocolate on each pillow.

* * *

Giselle wasn't quite clear on what they had done the night before, but her hangover let her know that alcohol had definitely been involved. She dragged herself out of bed to get to the Sunrise Pathway to Yoga class. She knew if she forced herself to do it, she would feel better afterwards. Lizbet was already awake and applying her Crème Ancienne face cream. Giselle slowly dressed and grabbed her Louis Vuitton Dhanura yoga bag and mat that she had brought with her. As she approached the cabin door to leave for her class, Lizbet gave her a perky wave. "We have lots of exciting activities planned for today! I'm heading out to my coconut milk wrap in just a few. See you at breakfast!" Giselle managed a less than enthusiastic wave as she departed.

In the next room, Kathryn and Brooke were working with an energetic instructor to achieve a flatter stomach, perfect posture, and a pain-free back, or so they had been told.

Chelsea was scheduled for the Reflexology Seminar. Carole agreed to go with her and learn how to work through the soles of the feet "to release *chi* to maintain positive mind, body and soul." Carole knew she could stand to release quite a bit of *chi*.

Madison and Sarah were sleeping in. They found a nice surprise on their door when they finally woke up. During the night, the cabin stewards had delivered a package for each of them from Giselle. With her partner, Giselle had designed a lightweight cotton waffle weave body wrap in what they called "One size fits most." The oversized pocket was embroidered with each woman's initial. Along with the wrap, each woman received a coordinated stretch headband to hold her hair in place during a facial or massage.

Giselle kept the Aquamarine color for herself. For the others she decided to give Chelsea the Sun Yellow, and Madison the Sky Blue. Carole received the Spearmint Green, and Sarah, the Sea Lavendar. Brooke's wrap was Apricot, and Kathryn's was Cobalt. Last, but never the least, Lizbet received a spa outfit in Petal Pink.

At breakfast, everyone present thanked Giselle for the outfits before Lizbet reminded everyone of their activities. For Madison and Sarah, who had skipped the meal, Lizbet had asked the steward to slip a note under their door with their schedule. Carefully prepared agendas in hand, the ladies headed off for different parts of the ship to get a therapeutic body massage, seaweed wrap, mud bath treatment or manicure.

After a light continental breakfast in her cabin, Madison sneaked over to the Internet Café to check her e-mail. She just couldn't stay unplugged. With a large mocha frappacino by her side, she plowed through the messages that had already accumulated. Next door to the Café, Sarah was in the library buried in an 800-page novel her friend Frances had recommended. This made her feel better than any of the spa treatments she saw listed.

Giselle, Chelsea and Carole met up at the solarium for a dip in the pool. Giselle was attracting quite a few looks with her latest bikini. Nearby, Kathryn, Lizbet and Brooke had the Thalassotherapy Pool to themselves. Featuring airbed recliner lounges, neck fountains, a waterfall, and body massage jet benches, it was the perfect place to relax. As Brooke and Kathryn leaned back on their recliner lounges and closed their eyes, Lizbet told them about a recent trip when she and Grant had stayed at

Hong Kong's Hotel Intercontinental. They had a 24-hour butler who shared with her the secret to drawing a relaxing bath. Lizbet confided, "Whenever I'm feeling particularly stressed, I ask Mrs. McGrath to draw a hot bath and add 3 drops each of peppermint, rosemary, eucalyptus and lavender essential oils. Then I just step into the tub and relax and breathe deeply for at least 15 minutes. When I'm finished, I sip a freshly brewed cup of mint tea. After a tiring day, this simple routine will always help me to feel rejuvenated."

Brooke murmured "Hmmm" to acknowledge she had heard Lizbet, but then quickly nodded off. Kathryn smiled dreamily as she moved her right hand slowly back and forth in the warm water. After a few quiet minutes, Lizbet rose and toweled off. She reminded everyone about the Captain's Formal Champagne reception at 7:30. She told them she was heading back to her cabin to watch the sunset from her balcony. Chelsea and Brooke decided to stay a little bit longer, but the others gathered their things from the chaises and headed back to their cabins to freshen up.

* * *

The energy of the group was revived at dinner. While nibbling a meringue cookie, Lizbet tried to get everyone interested in signing up for the talent show the next day.

Kathryn laughed. "No talent show for me. My talent is duty-free shopping."

Madison seconded the veto. "Don't even think about it, Lizbet."

Lizbet pouted. "Then how about the wine tasting?"

Giselle pushed aside her plate of half-eaten cheesecake and agreed. "That works for me." Carole, Chelsea, and Brooke said they were amenable. Madison told them that she and Sarah had already signed up for Bingo.

The others laughed. "Bingo?"

Sarah laughed too, but said, "I haven't played Bingo since the kids were little. C'mon, it will be fun."

The women reached a compromise. They'd play Bingo while drinking wine.

Still laughing, the group headed over to the piano bar for an after-dinner drink. Kathryn scooted next to Giselle so they could have a quiet word while they sipped their white cranberry martinis.

"So how is Carlo working out, Giselle?"

Flashing her thousand-watt smile, Giselle answered quickly, "The girls just adore him."

Kathryn smiled back. "What about Massimo?"

Giselle fidgeted with her drink. "What do you mean? What about Massimo?"

Kathryn took a sip of her martini. As she placed her oversized glass on the bar, she clarified the question. "Does Massimo just adore Carlo, too?"

Giselle looked over toward the piano player. "He really hasn't said. Carlo is really only at my house a few days a week, when I need an extra pair of hands."

"Yes, I know just how handy he is," Kathryn replied. "And what about you, Giselle, do you just adore him?"

Giselle avoided eye contact. "Kathryn, there is absolutely nothing going on between me and Carlo."

"Right."

"Really, he is just there to help me with the girls." Giselle asked the waiter for a refill.

"I'm sure that's true, Giselle. By the way, how is that birthmark of his? Did he ever get it removed?"

"Birthmark?"

Kathryn traced an imaginary circle on the table. "You know, the round birthmark on his forearm that was getting darker. He wanted to get it checked out."

Giselle fingered her blonde hair and looked confused. "He doesn't have a birthmark on his arm. It's on his thigh."

Kathryn smiled, and Giselle realized too late what she had said.

As Kathryn stood up and wished all a good night, Sarah asked for volunteers for an early morning jog on the outdoor track.

When no one responded, she asked again. "C'mon, doesn't anyone need exercise?"

Madison said she wanted to release some endorphins, but she didn't have the energy.

Chelsea tried to be helpful. "You've got a lot of energy, Madison. You kept up with me at paddle tennis last week, and you don't get to play nearly as often as I do."

Madison responded, "No offense, but you're not the most competitive person. I know a lot of others who could clean my clock—*if* I tried to keep up with them."

Chelsea addressed the group. "Speaking of competition, did you hear what happened at the paddle courts last week?"

Madison leaned forward. "No, I was traveling on business, and since I've been back I had so much to do to get ready for the cruise."

Chelsea took center stage. "Constance Phipps threw a fit when she found out which partner she'd been assigned."

Kathryn interjected, "Who did they give her as a partner?"

Chelsea laughed, "Me! You should have heard Constance complaining to her friend, Peyton, 'They tried to pair me with Chelsea, but I set them straight. Chelsea's a very nice person, but hardly at my level of ability.'"

Madison asked, "Did that really surprise you? You know Constance is serious about her winning. Don't you remember the time Siwanoy's tennis pro assigned her to the B team for tennis, so she withdrew and played at Shenorock since they were putting her on the A team?"

Chelsea lamented, "But I signed up because I wanted the exercise and to play for fun."

Brooke chimed in, "Don't worry, everyone's not like her. I'm not the greatest paddle tennis player, but I'd love to set up a date to play when we get back to Bronxville."

Carole suggested, "C'mon let's head back to the rooms. Lizbet has a busy day planned for us tomorrow."

Sarah whispered, "That's what I'm afraid of."

* * *

But the next day, their last, was actually a lot of laughs. In the morning four of them went to advanced napkin folding, while the other four learned everything anyone would want to know about towel folding. They all came together at lunch and compared notes. As Sarah tried in vain to fold the napkin into a bird, the way she had just learned, Lizbet cleared her throat. She told Sarah she would show her the right way to do it later. Now she wanted to tell them about her surprise.

There were some skeptical looks upon hearing the word "surprise." Lizbet could hardly contain her enthusiasm. After a dramatic pause, she explained, "I have arranged for us all to have a private session with a certified astrologer on board." She waited for cries of delight, but instead encountered blank stares.

"Ladies, this astrologer was on another cruise Grant and I took to Alaska, and believe me, she is a marvel. Not that I really believe in that kind of thing, of course, but I just think it would be such fun. Don't you all agree?"

They looked at each other, and the final consensus was, "Why not?" Lizbet clapped her freshly-moisturized hands in delight.

They took the elevators to the Lunar Lounge and entered the dark, hushed room. As they seated themselves, the astrologist, Farah, walked in through a side door and took her place at the head of the large round table.

Speaking in a deep voice, she asked the group, "Who wants to go first?"

At Lizbet's urging, Brooke volunteered.

In a low, serious voice, Farah asked her, "When's your birthday?"

"December 30."

Farah nodded solemnly. "Ah, a Capricorn. Well, you have many strengths. I'm sure you've been told that you are calm, persistent, careful, patient, loyal, and disciplined. Capricorns set high goals and have a need to do things right. If you commit to something, you always feel responsible for seeing it through."

As Brooke nodded, Farah continued. "Your horoscope for today is to get out and visit with friends, but don't tell them everything."

Brooke looked around the table. "Okay, everyone, you've been warned. I'm not telling you how much weight I've gained on this trip!"

Farah turned to Kathryn. "And when is your birthday?"

Kathryn told Farah that she was an Aquarius since her birthday was January 29.

Farah looked Kathryn in the eye. "You are a very friendly and idealistic person who has a strong sense of community. You are sympathetic and understanding and have great intuition. The word independent was invented to describe those born under the sign of Aquarius. You form your own opinion and if someone dares to push or pressure you, you will quickly show your stubborn side. You are hopeful and optimistic about the future, unpredictable, and not too concerned with public opinion. You have a very strong drive for adventure and freedom."

Kathryn nodded as Farah continued. "Your horoscope advises you to put more than your back into your job if you want to succeed. Put your heart into it too, and you'll find that it goes a lot faster."

Kathryn frowned. "That sounds like I've been sleeping with the boss, doesn't it?" She laughed, "Since my boss is most definitely a woman, it's a good thing everyone knows how much I like men!"

Farah ignored the comment and moved on to Madison, who didn't wait to be asked the question. "My birthday is November 25."

"Ah, a Scorpio. You are very charismatic, full of passion and intensity. You are like a detective whose analytical mind can probe far below the surface to look for motives. You are very tenacious and have tremendous willpower. You do well in positions of authority. Scorpios rule the eighth house of the chart."

Madison looked quizzical. "What exactly does that mean?"

"The eighth house is associated with other people's wealth."

Madison was beginning to think Farah knew what she was talking about. Farah continued with Madison's horoscope for the day. "As you're getting rid of the stuff you don't need, be sure to ask around. Something you've outgrown could be perfect for somebody else. Be generous."

Kathryn piped up. "How about that Art Deco brooch you showed us at La Grenouille. Have you outgrown that?"

Everyone laughed, except Lizbet and Farah. Lizbet shushed the others and asked Farah to do Chelsea's reading.

Chelsea volunteered, "I'm a Pisces. My birthday is March 4."

Farah gave the hint of a smile. "You are a bit of a dreamer. You are very imaginative, creative and artistic. Others tend to take advantage of your time and energy, leaving you to wonder why you're always so tired…You are romantic and sensitive and concerned with the feelings of others. You are very empathetic and strive to help people less fortunate than you."

Chelsea thought Farah was right on the money. "What's my horoscope for today?"

"You're good at providing for others without even being asked. Let someone return the favor."

Chelsea turned to the others. "Okay, who wants to do me a favor?"

Giselle offered, "I'll take you to my stylist to get you a new hairdo."

As Chelsea put her hands on her hips in mock horror at Giselle's kind offer, Giselle waved her hand at Farah. "How about me? My birthday is April 28. What does that make me?"

Kathryn opened her mouth to speak, but thought better of it.

Farah told Giselle, "You are very sensual, warm-hearted and always available to listen to a friend's problem and give advice. You are persistent in working towards your goals. This sometimes makes you a bit stubborn once you've made up your mind about something. With friends and partners, the Taurus can be jealous and possessive."

Giselle wasn't sure she wanted to hear more, but Farah wasn't finished.

"Comfort and luxury are very important to you. You are always looking for harmony and inner peace. You do have a few weaknesses. You can be somewhat inflexible and deaf to any kind of criticism. Allow yourself a break. Your place should be looking nice by now, so play host. A nice dinner for you and loved ones would be welcome."

Giselle pouted. "I like the luxury and harmony part, but inflexible and resistant to criticism? I don't think so. And no more dinners for a while. Massimo won't let me wear my French maid costume in public since that dinner we hosted for the Silent Auction."

Lizbet's turn was next. "Farah, my birthday is March 31, and I am an Aries."

Farah told her she could tell. "Arians are dynamos of energy when they set their mind on achieving a goal. They are ready for action and achievement, so don't get in their way."

Lizbet liked it so far. "Tell me more."

"You are very enthusiastic, and your enthusiasm is infectious. You get involved in something and get others to follow. Some Aries are described as having a need to control others. But other Aries view themselves as merely self-confident individuals who need to take charge to face challenges quickly and forcefully. Aries are very competitive and are known for clearing obstacles out of their path."

Carole said, "I heard they can be impatient."

Farah agreed. "Yes, they might act impulsively and forget that others might see things differently. If those people don't share the Aries' point of view, watch out!"

Lizbet thanked Carole for her input and asked Farah for the day's horoscope.

Farah told her she would be pleased. "You will have success at last! Don't bask too long in the glory, though. New challenges wait."

Lizbet glowed. "Success, I knew it! Don't worry, ladies, I won't rub it in when Whitney gets accepted to her first choice college. My only challenge will be making sure her new Yale blue Beemer can be delivered as soon as we get the thick envelope."

Sarah was next in line. "I don't like the name of my sign. It's Cancer. My birthday is June 25."

Farah told Sarah that "Cancerians have a natural empathy that causes them to worry too much about everyone else's problems and feelings. You are highly sensitive, nurturing, sentimental and thoughtful. You make your home a safe and protected place for your loved ones. Your moodiness causes you to be on top of the world one moment and down in the pits the next."

Sarah thought about what Farah said as she told her the day's horoscope. "You're very attractive today, in a self-assured, smoldering way. Continue taking care of what you have to get done, but make time for a romantic interlude."

Giselle mentioned that Massimo was Cancer, too. "He'd better not be *romantically interluding* with anyone while I'm away."

Kathryn countered, "How about if he carries on while you're home?"

Before it could go any further, Carole quickly spoke up. "I was born on September 4. What about my sign?"

Farah consulted her chart. "You are modest, reserved and practical."

Carole looked incredulous. "Me?"

"Yes, but that doesn't stop you from participating in lively discussions to express your ideas. You're also a hard worker who has little tolerance for others who don't share your work ethic. You are serious, efficient, and detail oriented, and this causes you to sometimes miss the big picture. You're a perfectionist and sometimes…"

"Did Andrew tell you to say that?"

"I beg your pardon?"

Carole waved her hand. "Nothing, please continue."

"Sometimes your nervous energy sends you into fits of worry. Some of your relationships might suffer if you can't resist the urge to be overly critical or complaining."

Carole asked if the stars had any good news for her.

Farah told her, "You're a person who can handle a lot of details. You're pretty good with distractions, too, and you're getting better with practice."

"I have been a little distracted lately. I have a lot on my mind."

Giselle said, "Well, this has been fun, but I know what's on my mind now. Who wants to go shopping?"

Lizbet thanked Farah and waited for her to leave.

As they filed out of the room, Lizbet told Giselle, "I'll go shopping with you. I need that tanzanite and diamond necklace. I know Grant would want me to have it for our anniversary."

Chelsea also wanted to go to the boutiques. "I want to buy that Breitling watch for Ted. He could use another casual watch for weekend wear."

Carole said she could look for some perfume for Andrew's girls. "I'm not sure they'll appreciate it, but I really am trying. And now I know why Andrew might think I'm overly critical or complaining when it comes to the girls. When I get home, I'm going to tell him it's not my fault...it's in the stars."

Giselle wanted to pick up the stuffed sailor bears for Lily and perfume for Hannah. Brooke agreed. "That's a good idea...I'll get those for my girls, too."

Kathryn realized, "I'd better get something for Pryce, too, but a bear isn't going to cut it. Let's go see what the shops have so we can clean them out before dinner."

Madison hated shopping with a passion, so she convinced Sarah to hang out by the pool and do absolutely nothing...that is, once she checked her e-mail.

* * *

Dinner was lively as the women celebrated their last night at sea. Champagne flowed and promises to do this again soon were made by all. As they rose to leave the restaurant, Lizbet thanked the wait staff on behalf of the entire group and handed each of them an envelope.

Still in high spirits, the ladies paused on the grand staircase outside the dining room to have a group photo taken. Lizbet checked her reflection in one of the mirrored columns flanking the staircase. Her new Nicole Miller strapless gown looked stunning, if she did say so herself. Giselle was busy making sure her Tahari drape-neck silk dress was hugging her curves in all the right places.

The Italian photographer told the ladies that he never asked his subjects to say "Cheese." As he lined them up, he instructed each to think of something that always made them smile.

Brooke smiled beatifically as she thought about going "Home Sweet Home."

Sarah dreamed about the romantic interlude Farah predicted.

Carole loved animals, but she was thinking how happy she would be if she found out that the rabbit died when she returned to Bronxville.

Madison smiled at the 126 point rise in the Dow she had spied flickering across the CNN screen in the bar.

Chelsea grinned at the thought of seeing her two boys when they got home from school the next day.

Lizbet missed the part about thinking it to herself, so she smiled and said "Yale" out loud.

Kathryn tried to think about Trip, but instead had nostalgic visions of "Carlo." There was something about the photographer that reminded her of her former Manny.

Next to her, Giselle struck her signature runway pose and tried to think about Massimo. But it was futile. As she gazed alluringly into the camera, Giselle shared Kathryn's vision…it was just so much more exciting.

"I don't know much about being a millionaire, but I'll bet I'd be darling at it."

Dorothy Parker

Chapter 10

Deck the halls with boughs of holly!

~ ~ ~

Usher in the season with a tour of some of the most spectacular homes in our village. The stockings will be hung from the chimney with care, chestnuts will be roasting on an open fire, and a turkey and some mistletoe will help to make the season bright.

Tour festive homes throughout the village that are all decked out for the holidays. Be sure not to miss the final stop on the tour hosted by Grant and Lizbet Wellington Smith. Sip champagne, nibble hors d'oeuvres, and sing along with the Victorian carolers as they help to make the spirit bright.

December 10
3:00–7:00 p.m.
Bid: $125 per person fixed
Maximum: 150 tickets
Tour the Homes of:

Cordelia and Oliver Wilkinson IV
Wright and Danica Corbett
Ellison and Judith Lewellyn
George and Pamela Connaught
Grant and Lizbet Wellington Smith

~ ~ ~

*A*fter a brief stop at the stone and shingle Victorian style home designed for Elizabeth Bacon Custer, widow of General George Armstrong Custer, Brooke and Kathryn headed over to Pondfield Road. They definitely didn't want to be late for the gathering at the Smiths, the last stop on the tour.

It was fortunate that Grant and Lizbet lived next door to Brooke and Morgan. Since parking on the nearby side streets was already congested, Brooke was able to pull her Beemer into her own circular driveway for safekeeping. As Kathryn stepped out of the car, the simple beauty of Morgan and Brooke's decorations momentarily distracted her. All of the diamond-paned, leaded glass windows were lit by small white candles that emitted a soft glow. The archway leading to the terrace was entwined with garlands of fragrant evergreens and mixed hollies. Affixed to the oak front door was a large wreath made with oregonia and cedar with accents of dried hydrangea and miniature pinecones. Instead of the traditional red, Brooke had her florist attach a luxurious forest green velvet bow. Just to the left of the flagstone terrace at the side of the house, two lighted reindeer were grazing and gracefully lifting and turning their heads in electronic choreography. Kathryn complimented Brooke on how exquisite the decorations were as she followed Brooke over to the Smiths.

As Kathryn and Brooke approached Lizbet's imposing stone mansion, they noticed two smartly dressed women checking the copper address marker affixed to one of the large pillars at the foot of the walkway. Brooke assured the women that they were at the right place—1988 Elm Rock Road. No matter how many times she saw the Smith's house, Kathryn was still impressed with how dramatic the house looked as one approached the stone turret entry. Neither Brooke nor Kathryn had been inside since Lizbet had it professionally decorated for the holidays, but both were sure it would be nothing less than spectacular.

Mrs. McGrath opened the massive front door with the stained glass panel and ushered them in. Brooke deftly side-stepped the oversized eucalyptus and pepperberry kissing ball and moved over by the 6-foot nutcracker. She picked up a pair of the hospital booties all tour participants were required to wear. As she sat on a window seat in the two-story entry hall to don the booties, Brooke noticed that throughout the first floor rooms, as far as she could see, masses of crimson and white poinsettias were artfully arranged. Chelsea had supplied pots of Schlumbergera—Christmas cactus to landscaping novices—in hues of salmon, fuschia and white that lined the low, deep window ledges immediately to her left.

As more guests entered behind them, Brooke, Kathryn and others who had arrived at the same time, moved into the 18-foot high formal living room. As the guests stepped down into the living room, their eyes were drawn to the enormous Scotch pine tree decorated with hand-painted mouth-blown glass ornaments. The luxurious velvet tree skirt was monogrammed with the Smith family crest. Circling around the immense tree was a set of O-gauge Lionel trains that included a sleek black 2332 Pennsylvania locomotive—with working headlight—that whistled and puffed smoke as it steamed along the tracks pulling a milk car, barrel car, boxcar with moveable doors, and caboose. There was enough room for an elaborate set-up of trestles, bridges, and switches as the trains headed to the nostalgic railroad station. Beyond the train tracks, silver and gold foil-wrapped packages topped with sheer organdy ribbon, tiny faux-berry wreaths, and beaded snowflakes were heaped under the tree. Off to the side of the octagonal-shaped room, a fire was blazing beneath the hand-embroidered stockings for Grant, Lizbet and Whitney. Over the fireplace, an oil painting of the family, and their golden retriever, Yale, were captured in a formal casual pose.

Gripping the mahogany balustrade of the imposing staircase at the far end of the room, Lizbet made a grand entrance to greet her visitors. At the foot of the wide stairway she paused and unobtrusively smoothed her floor-length tartan plaid taffeta skirt with gold metallic thread that she had paired with a feminine black velvet top with sweeping bateau neckline. Her ash blonde hair was held back with a red velvet headband with snow-white marabou trim. On her size-6 feet, she wore black velvet ballet slippers with a red velvet bow. As only she could, Lizbet managed to achieve a look that was both classic and modern. Fortunately for him, Grant was still in the city or Lizbet would have insisted that he wear the satin smoking jacket and velvet bedroom slippers she had given him last Christmas. It was not purely accidental that he suddenly had an important client meeting on the same day as the house tour.

Lizbet led the assembled entourage into the dining room. The white-linen covered dining table (with a perfect red "S" monogrammed on the perfectly mitered corner) was set for a holiday dinner with Tiffany china, silver, and crystal champagne flutes. Each place setting had a tiny ornament place card holder with the name of the guest in elaborate calligraphy. The center of the long rectangular table held a collection of cache pots with festive amaryllis surrounded by variegated ficus that were sent over by Chelsea. Her accompanying note to Lizbet explained the particular varieties of the amaryllis she had chosen for the occasion: *Carnival*, its white petals striped with red, reminded one of candy canes; *Wedding Dance* with its white star shaped flowers; and *Pamela*, a miniature variety with brilliant red flowers. Above the centerpiece, Swarovski star ornaments on white satin ribbons hung from the custom made eighteen-arm Waterford crystal chandelier.

At the far end of the dining room, the Federal sideboard held the large sterling silver punch bowl ready for holiday guests to quench their thirst. The bowl was surrounded with holly-studded evergreens and boughs of pine tied with red plaid ribbon. An ornately-carved silver tray laden with intricately decorated gingerbread men was too irresistible. Although the dining room was made to appear as if the holiday dinner guests were just about to arrive, the actual refreshments for the tour guests were to be served in the library and main ballroom. But Brocke was so hungry. She had barely had time after her shift as a volunteer at the Christmas tree sale for the Children's Adoption Services to change into fresh clothes for the Holiday House Tour. One cookie wouldn't be missed. When she was sure no one was looking, she surreptitiously lifted a cookie and took a bite. She almost choked. Couldn't someone have told her these were prop cookies covered in shellac?! As Lizbet turned at the sound of coughing, Brooke recovered quickly, smiling gamely while attempting to hide the broken body of the gingerbread man in a bright green napkin that declared "Happy Holidays from the Smiths!"

Continuing on through the library, the guests headed into the grand ballroom for caroling around the Steinway piano. Kathryn and Brooke paused to pick up a glass of Moet & Chandon Brut champagne offered by waiters in black vests and red bow ties. As the women found a spot over by the fireplace, Victorian carolers entered through a side door. The entertainment began with the singing of many old favorites, including *Deck the Halls, The Twelve Days of Christmas,* and of course, *Jingle Bells.* Following the caroling, there was a brief intermission while a group of Julliard students took their places. To start the program, a baritone appeared at one of the balconies overlooking the ballroom and led off with his moving interpretation of "Der Vogelfanger bin ich ja" by Wolfgang Amadeus Mozart and followed up with "Rheinlegendchem" by Gustav Mahler. The other musicians, on the main floor of the ballroom, playing the flute, violin, viola and cello then performed an enchanting version of Mozart's Flute Quartet in D major. A soprano, tenor, baritone and pianist ended the program with *What Child is This, The First Noel, and Silent Night.* While all present applauded enthusiastically as the last note sounded, Mrs.

McGrath entered the library followed by a group of middle school girls in velvet and taffeta dresses carrying trays of hors d'ouvres.

Brooke ducked into the powder room. Even this room was decorated down to the most minute detail. Brooke disposed of the remains of her gingerbread man in a wastebasket trimmed with a wide silver ribbon. Glittering icicles that caught the light were suspended from the antique sconces that flanked the antique oval mirror rimmed with silver beading. The vanity held an Ivy topiary adorned with miniature angel soaps. After washing her hands, Brooke reached for the one of the white fingertip towels embroidered with silver bells.

Brooke found Kathryn in the living room, talking with several of the book club members who had just arrived. Brooke smiled at Carole and wished her a Merry Christmas. She wondered if it was her imagination, or was Carole looking a little green around the gills. Brooke supposed it had something to do with the fact that one of the homes on the tour belonged to Andrew's ex-wife Alexandra. That must have been difficult for Carole. Brooke tried to keep the conversation light and asked how Carole's fundraising job was going, and about her plans for the holiday. In the middle of their hellos, Carole quickly excused herself and ran towards the bathroom Brooke had just vacated. Seeing the look of concern on Brooke's face, Kathryn explained that there was no need to worry, Carole was fine. In fact, better than fine. She and Andrew had just found out that they were expecting a baby and she was happily experiencing "morning" sickness, which any woman who had ever been pregnant knew could happen at any time throughout the day. It would most definitely be a Merry Christmas and an especially Happy New Year for Carole.

Carole returned looking a little less pale and all the women embraced her and gave their heartfelt congratulations. Sarah and Madison were especially thrilled. It had been a long time since either of them had held a new baby. They both agreed on one piece of advice for the prospective mother…Get as much sleep as you can now. They warned her that in a few months, sleep would definitely be a luxury.

Sarah asked what Andrew's girls' thought of the news.

Carole shook her head in disbelief. "Believe it or not, they actually seem to be happy about it. I thought they might be jealous, but so far, they seem to be really excited about the news. Andrew thinks they're probably thinking that we won't have as much time to "interfere" in their business, since we'll be spending a lot of time taking care of a new baby. I'm not sure they'll ever volunteer to baby-sit, but I'm just glad they're not giving us a hard time. I really want to enjoy every minute of my pregnancy."

While Carole listened to maternity advice from Sarah, Kathryn and Madison, Giselle and Brooke drifted over by the fireplace and discussed their recent trips to the city. Brooke had arranged for front-row tickets for herself, Morgan, Charlotte and Jayne to see the Nutcracker at Lincoln Center. It was magnificent. Too bad Spencer hadn't wanted to accompany them. Charlotte and Jayne had been entranced by the classic performance featuring the original 1892 Russian choreography by Lev Ivanov and Marius Petipa. The costumes had been colorful; the set design, amazing; and the Tchaikovsky score, absolutely superb. Giselle had taken Hannah and Lily to see the Radio City Christmas Spectacular. Giselle had been pleasantly surprised at just how "spectacular" the show had been. Brooke asked Giselle what Massimo thought of the production.

With conversations going on all around them, Kathryn overheard only parts of Giselle and Brooke's exchange. She strained to hear how Giselle would respond to the question about Massimo. Carole might be a little pregnant, but the pause from Giselle was completely pregnant.

Giselle fidgeted with her drink. "Well, Massimo couldn't make it this year."

Kathryn joined the women as Brooke commiserated that it was too bad Massimo had missed the show this time, but hopefully next year he'd be able to go with them.

"Well, he probably won't be going with us next year, either," Giselle said quietly. "You see, we've separated."

Brooke grasped Giselle's hand. "I am so sorry. I feel so stupid. I didn't know."

"It's okay, really. I'm not sure what happened. I guess we both just kind of grew apart and before I knew it…"

Kathryn was genuinely saddened at the news. With excuses to Brooke, she pulled Giselle to the side. "Giselle, are you sure about this? Massimo is a great guy and a terrific father. You guys belong together. Carlo is just not worth it. Believe me, I know what I'm talking about."

"Well, whether I'm sure about it or not, it's done. Apparently I'm not the only one who's been having second thoughts about our marriage. Massimo moved out just after we got back from the cruise. He's moved his stuff into an apartment at the Avalon."

Kathryn touched Giselle's arm. "I really am sorry. This has to be awfully hard on the girls."

Giselle nodded. "It hasn't really sunk in yet. He's still close enough that they see him a lot, but obviously it's not the same."

Kathryn looked Giselle in the eye. "Giselle, I'm sure if you try, you and Massimo can still work this out. The first thing you've got to do is get rid of Carlo. Show the bum the door."

Giselle laughed. "Oh, you don't have to worry about Carlo. You were right about him all along. He was only interested in me when I was hard to get. Once Massimo moved out, Carlo moved on. Unfortunately, Massimo has also been stepping out. I hear he's been seeing an awful lot of a new young model his agency just signed."

Kathryn commiserated with her friend. She knew how it felt to be left for the newest flavor of the month.

Giselle looked confused. "I don't know what I'm going to do. I really thought I knew what I wanted, but now I'm not so sure. And it seems as if Massimo isn't sure either." She wiped a tear away and put her arm through Kathryn's. "C'mon, it's the holidays and I'm not about to let the Grinch steal Christmas."

As Giselle and Kathryn walked over to rejoin their friends, Francesca came into the room. It had been a while since Francesca had seen her friends, and she hurried through the crowd to reach them. She regretted that she had been unable to spend the day with them at Tiffany's, or sail away into the Atlantic Ocean for a long weekend. But she felt strongly that she needed to set a good example for the kids. As a teacher, she was blessed with a lot of time off, and she rarely took a day off while classes were in session. After much hugging, Francesca offered her congratulations to Kathryn. Houlihan Lawrence had just been announced as the winner of the annual Bronxville Chamber of Commerce's Window Display Contest. Their miniature recreation of a Victorian mansion was sensational and everyone knew that Kathryn had overseen the entire effort.

Madison added her congratulations and noted that Kathryn looked especially gorgeous. Beautifully dressed in a smart black crepe sheath adorned by a simple gold choker, Kathryn gracefully accepted the kudos while also giving thanks for the body shaper she wore under her form-fitting dress. Maybe she should just give in and have liposuction. On the other hand, plastic surgery hadn't exactly improved Giselle's life.

Sarah and Madison moved off near a table by the window that held a collection of tabletop trees including rosemary, cypress, and ivy arranged on a red and white plaid runner. "So, Madison, are you ready for the holidays?"

Madison didn't bat an eye. "I've outsourced Christmas this year."

Sarah laughed. "How can you outsource Christmas?"

Madison explained. "Look, I'm so busy at work this time of year, and John is too. We have no idea what Cole wants. So we hired a personal shopper who finds the perfect presents for everyone on our list."

Sarah looked skeptical.

"Don't give me that look, Sarah. You know perfectly well that shopping puts me in a less than jovial mood. It's just not in my genes. It's worth the $250 an hour fee that I have to pay to have someone else handle it for me."

"You sound like you need a little Christmas cheer." Sarah reached into her purse and pulled out a copy of an e-mail from a former colleague who thought she might be missing the corporate world. "Read this."

To: All Employees
From: Colby Sutton, Sr. Human Resources Director
Date: November 20
Re: Company Christmas Party

Colleagues, save the date for the company's Christmas party which will take place on December 23 at noon at the Regency Café. Please note that this annual affair is for employees only. There will be a buffet lunch and cash bar with plenty to drink! We have arranged for a wonderful quartet to sing traditional carols…please feel free to sing along as we light the tree and rejoice in the holiday spirit.

Following our sumptuous lunch, our very own VP of Marketing will make an appearance as Santa Claus to begin the exchange of gifts! Please note that no gift should be over $10.00, thereby making the giving of gifts easier on everyone's pockets.

I'd like to be the first to wish you and your family a very Merry Christmas.

Warmest Regards,

Colby

To: All Employees
From: Colby Sutton, Sr. Human Resources Director
Date: November 21
Re: Holiday Party

Colleagues, yesterday's memo certainly was not intended to exclude our Jewish or Pagan employees. Although we recognize that Chanukah and Saturnalia are important holidays that often coincide with Christmas, unfortunately that was not the case this year. Therefore, to avoid this situation in the future, henceforth we will refer to our annual gathering as the "Holiday Party."

Also, for those of you who were concerned, rest assured, there will be no Christmas tree in evidence at the restaurant, and no Christmas carols will be permitted. We will have Muzak piped in for your listening pleasure while you eat.

One additional reminder. In compliance with our company's harassment policy, please be sure refrain from commenting on anyone who has donned gay apparel as it might be deemed offensive by some of your fellow employees.

Again, Happy Holidays to you and your family.

Best regards,

Colby

To: All Employees
From: Colby Sutton, Sr. Human Resources Director
Date: November 22
Re: Holiday Party

    Everyone, please disregard the previous notice about the gift exchange. There are to be no gifts exchanged during the party.

    The union members feel that $10.00 is too much money, unless management contributes at least $8.52 per member to share the cost of the gift. Management believes that $10.00 is too chintzy and wants to raise the amount to $15.00, but will only agree to contribute $3.28 per member towards the cost. Since it is unlikely this issue can be arbitrated before the party, NO GIFT EXCHANGE WILL BE ALLOWED.

Regards,

Colby

To: All Employees
From: Colby Sutton, Sr. Human Resources Director
Date: November 23
Re: Holiday Party

Aren't we a diverse group! I wish I had been informed earlier that December 20 begins the holy month of Ramadan, which forbids eating and drinking during daylight hours. Since a luncheon would not accommodate our Muslim employees' beliefs, I have contacted the Regency Café and asked them to provide any employee who wishes the option of having the meal at the end of the party; alternatively, they may request a festive, nondenominational doggy bag.

Also, I have arranged for members of Weight Watchers, Jenny Craig and the newly formed Atkins Club to sit farthest from the gala dessert buffet. Since I am unable to monitor the salt used in the preparation of food, one person at each table will be designated to test the food for the others who might have high blood pressure. Pregnant women will be assigned to the table closest to the Ladies Room. Gays are permitted to sit with each other; however, if we have enough requests, we can accommodate one table for the Gay men and a separate table for the Lesbian women. Unfortunately, at this point we do not have enough requests to set aside a table for cross dressers. For the vertically challenged, we will have booster seats available. For the member of Alcoholics Anonymous who sent me an unsigned note requesting an alcohol-free table, I'm sure you can understand that if I post an "AA only" sign, the employees who choose to sit at that table wouldn't be anonymous anymore.

If I've overlooked anything, please don't hesitate to contact me.
C.

To: All Employees
From: Colby Sutton, Sr. Human Resources Director
Date: November 24
Re: Goddamn Holiday Party

Of course, how could I have forgotten about you vegans? Well, guess what, people? You can sit right next to the roast beef carving table…I really don't give a flying $#@*!

And to the people who left voice mails for my secretary asking when the taxi vouchers would be available, all of you can forget about getting any of those this year since the odor of the air fresheners in the car service we use might offend someone. Drink and drive for all I care.

C.

To: All Employees
From: Karen Davis, Interim Human Resources Director
Date: November 27
Re: Holiday Party

I'm sure I speak for all of us in wishing Colby Sutton a speedy recovery. Since it's unlikely she'll be back before the new year, I'll forward your wishes for a healthy and happy holiday season to her.

In the meantime, management has voted to cancel our Holiday Party and give everyone the afternoon of the 23rd off with full pay.

Happy Holidays!
Karen

Madison refused to give Sarah the papers back. "I have to show these to John. He needs a good laugh. He is actually living this at his company right now. He's so fed up. He says that saying *Merry Christmas* at the office is almost as bad as using a four letter word." Sarah knew exactly what she meant—yet one more reason she did not miss the corporate world.

As Madison tucked the e-mails into her bag, she pulled out the holiday cards she had stuffed into her tote earlier in the day. "You think the corporate world you left is so bad? Well, I still haven't stopped laughing from this holiday missive we just got from one of your fellow 'retirees' from the corporate jungle. I hardly know this woman—I think we met at some school board or library function, but…"

Sarah grabbed the red paper from her friend's hands and began reading from the top, just under the graphic of the adorable five candy canes representing each member of the Richman family.

Merry, Merry Christmas!!!!!!!

This year was just chock full of good things for the Richman family!

It's so hard to believe, but all of our children—Cameron, Caitlyn and Court—are finally out of the baby stage. (Cooper has been told that this time I really mean it when I say No!).

Cameron reached his milestone birthday over the summer (yes, he really turned 5!) and headed off to kindergarten in the fall. We were so proud when we got the news that he was accepted at Phillips Academy, a private school about 25 minutes away. Although we hadn't planned to send him to private school yet, when we went up for a visit, Cam just fell I love with the place. So what's a parent to do! Cameron absolutely adores his teacher, Mrs. Sweet, and has made so many, many friends in his short time there. He swam like a fish all summer; that is, when he wasn't hitting tennis balls or playing the back nine at the Club with Cooper.

Caitlyn turned 3 in September. Her toddler years seem so long ago. She goes to the Early Childhood Center at Sarah Lawrence College five afternoons a week, and spends the mornings sketching and painting. Over the summer she took up skating. (Did someone say Olympics?) She's started skating lessons after school with a trainer, and she is a natural! She's always been quite the athlete. You should see her ride the new Schwinn Speedster mountain bike she got for her birthday. No training wheels for this girl!

Court celebrated his 2nd birthday on October 1, and since then hasn't given even a backwards glance at his babyhood. He sleeps in his big boy bed, drinks only from a cup, and uses the same full-sized silverware as the rest of the family! He graduated from his swimming class with honors (when he was still 1) and began tennis lessons in September. He spends two mornings a week at the Eliza Frost Child Center where he immediately charmed all his teachers. He is growing so fast! Court can't wait for Santa this year. He's hoping for new skis, and we have inside information from the big man himself that Court won't be disappointed! Not surprisingly, Court's added a new phrase to his rapidly increasing vocabulary—ski bum. It sounds so adorable when he says it.

Besides keeping up with her very active brood, Camilla's been quite busy with her own activities since leaving her executive position with Random House at the beginning of the year. But just when Cammie was starting to enjoy the freedom that came from not having such a demanding job, her old tennis injury flared up. But as those who know her well will tell you, nothing keeps Cammie down. She is following the doctor's exercises and is determined to ski with little Court in Aspen! She continues to pine for her corner office on Park Avenue, but she's figuring out new challenges to pursue that will still allow her to keep her big blue eyes on the kids and the staff at home.

Cooper spent so much quality time with the family this year thanks to his successful resolution of his discussions with Goldman Sachs. Of course he was thrilled that they agreed to his request to leave the company. He was happy to help them with a critical research project they gave him while they finalized the terms of his leaving. With his wealth of experience, the project really didn't take up too much of his time, so he was happy to do them that one last favor. Now that we have the luxury of so, so much together time, we're trying to figure out what Cooper's next move should be. Not that we don't love having him around, but it would be such a waste of his tremendous talents if he didn't pursue another executive position appropriate for someone of his caliber.

Lastly, we want to update all of you on the latest news about Chesterfield. Chesterfield underwent an extensive facelift in the spring and looks terrific. For those of you who haven't visited our summer home in a while, please make plans to come by and see Chesterfield's new and improved facade. It's truly incredible.

Looking ahead, we are excited about the new year and the possibilities that await the Richman family. Since Cooper has a bit more time on his hands now, we are thinking about expanding our annual holiday letter for next year. As a special thank you to you, our dear friends, from now on we will send you a special bonus with our annual letter—a DVD with video highlights of the most memorable Richman family moments from the entire year. There's always so much to share.

Love to all,

Cooper, Camilla,

Cameron, Caitlyn and Court Richman

Madison waited for Sarah to finish. "So, what was that you said about not missing the corporate world one bit? If the stay-at-home world had an organization chart, this woman would be Vice President in charge of the Stepford Wives' Trust."

Sarah laughed. "Touché!"

Madison laughed with her and then eagerly changed the subject. "How is Ruthann doing at Georgetown?"

Sarah lit up. "She's doing great. She is so happy, and as you know, when your kids are happy, all is right with the world. How is Cole coping with senior year?"

Madison also visibly brightened. "He's doing amazingly well. He understands that at this point he's done everything possible and he has to try to chill out and wait for the mail. I just hope Lizbet doesn't corner me about the status of Cole's college applications. I know Cole shared with Ruthann that he's doing Yale's Early Action option, so I'm not telling any tales out of school that he should hear any day. Maybe then we can all get a good night's sleep. I'm not sure if Whitney decided to Early Action or not, but if Cole receives a "thick" envelope and Whitney doesn't, our friend Lizbet will not take it well. She'll probably immediately file suit against the outrageously expensive college consultant they had hired to "assist" Whitney with her application."

Sarah said that in another year or so Dylan would be entering the wonderful world of PSAT's, SAT's, AP's and too many other letters of the alphabet she had come to dread. She bemoaned the fact that time was moving much too quickly. Even a simple thing like a pediatrician appointment was cause for anxiety these days. Dylan was outgrowing the pediatrician, but Sarah wasn't sure she was ready to outgrow being the mother of a son who needed a pediatrician.

Madison tried to reassure Sarah that not only would she get over Dylan's becoming more independent, she might also enjoy her own newfound freedom. As they continued their conversation, they could see Chelsea in the entry hall talking to Cece, the landscape designer who had arranged most of the flowers and greenery outside Lizbet's home. Chelsea and Cece had met the previous year at a cocktail party at the New York Botanical Gardens. At the reception in the Palm conservatories, the two women sipped chardonnay and marveled as model trains maneuvered through a miniature New York City made almost entirely of natural plant materials. With the best of intentions, they had vowed to keep in touch, but it just never seemed to happen. Chelsea generously praised her peer on the exquisite job she had done weaving faux greenery in with the fresh greens over the entryway. They both were sensing that more clients who wanted to *go faux.* Not only did it make the clean up effort less "prickly," it also was an investment that could be used year after year. Both women had also noticed the increasing use of fresh fruits in holiday displays—baskets of greens with pears and apples, cranberry garlands, and winterberry wreaths and candle rings.

Slowly, the guests were starting to disperse. Lizbet positioned herself near the front door to wish everyone a happy holiday. She saw Carole approaching and moved quickly to embrace her. "I just heard you're pregnant!"

Carole looked amazed. "News really does travel quickly, doesn't it?"

"Don't think you can keep anything from me! I can't wait to hear all about your plans. Are you going to keep working? Is Andrew happy? Do you have any names picked out? Which nursery school are you thinking about applying to?"

"Lizbet, I'm only two month's pregnant. We'll make a date for lunch and I'll fill you in on all the details."

"I'm going to hold you to that, *Mom.*"

Other guests noisily made their way over to where Lizbet was standing to thank her for a terrific event. Brooke approached and added her sincere thanks. "I can't wait for next year's Silent Auction. I'm just disappointed this is the last item that Morgan bought. Maybe next year I'll get him to donate some tickets to the MTV Awards and an after-party with some of his more interesting clients."

Lizbet kissed Brooke goodbye and told her, "I will definitely take you up on your offer. I can't wait to get started planning some new events."

Two of the last guests to depart were Madison and Sarah. Lizbet thanked them for coming and then took Madison's hand in hers.

"Madison, how are you holding up with the whole college process?"

"Actually, Lizbet, I'm holding up just fine, but I'm not the one who's waiting to hear where I'll be going to school next fall, Cole is. The process may not be perfect, but I truly believe that things work out for a reason, and if Cole doesn't get in to the first school on his list, there are others he's looked at that will give him a terrific college experience."

Lizbet attempted to look nonchalant. "Whitney doesn't seem concerned at all. It's as if she's at peace. I think she's just very confident she'll get into her first choice. I do hope she's not disappointed."

Sarah chimed in. "Whitney is a terrific young woman. I have no doubt she'll do just fine. Try not to worry."

Lizbet turned back to Madison. "I just hope too many of the other seniors aren't very disappointed. These schools are just so competitive. It's not enough to be brilliant anymore. These kids need every extra edge they can get. By the way, do you happen to know how many in the class are applying to, say Princeton? or Harvard? or Yale?"

Madison shook her head. "Happily, I don't know. These kids are under enough pressure without everybody constantly hounding them about how many AP courses did they take, which colleges they are applying to, which friends are they competing with, and so on. It will be a relief when Cole gets his letters and can put this whole part of the process behind him."

"So, he hasn't heard anything yet...no early decision letter from any school?"

"Sorry, Lizbet. If you want to know if he applied Early Decision to Yale, you'll have to ask him. I'm respecting his 'Don't Ask, Don't Tell' policy until all this is over."

Lizbet smiled sweetly. "Of course, I would never pry. I just wish the mailman would hurry up and bring me that thick envelope we're expecting. We should hear this month."

Madison touched Lizbet's arm.

"Lizbet, like Sarah said, try not to worry. 'Tis the season to be jolly."

As Lizbet turned to say good bye to her other guests, she said gaily, "Fa la la la la, la la la la, ladies!"

"When they discover the center of the universe, a lot of people will be disappointed to discover they are not it."

Bernard Bailey

Epilogue

The Essay

The Silent Auction

itsy called Lizbet to give her warning that she was coming over. Lizbet pleaded a migraine, but Bitsy was not taking "No" for an answer.

As Bitsy waited at the stop sign at Elm Rock, Kathryn's car pulled out of Brooke's driveway and approached from the other direction. Kathryn pulled up next to her and lowered her window. "Hello, Bitsy. It's good to see you. Brooke and I were just saying we hadn't seen you or Lizbet around lately. How are our favorite Gamma Gamma Girlfriends?"

"Great!" Bitsy chirped. "I'm just stopping by to say hello to Lizbet. Love to chat, but gotta run. See you soon!"

Bitsy accelerated, turned into Lizbet's driveway, and pulled her black onyx Lexus under the port cochere. She grabbed her purse and hopped out.

Mrs. McGrath opened the massive front door and led her into the library where her friend was curled up on a Wing chair.

"Lizbet, you simply must tell me what's wrong. I am one of your oldest friends, your closest sorority sister, and I can't bear to see you so unhappy. For goodness sake, ever since the holidays you have just not been yourself. You didn't show up at the fashion show luncheon yesterday...I heard you cancelled your hair appointment with José this morning...you're still not dressed…and now you tell me you don't even want to go shopping today. What on earth is wrong?"

Without a word, Lizbet rose and went over to the antique rolltop desk and picked up a tear-stained paper. As she handed it to her friend, Bitsy realized it was a copy of Whitney's application to Yale.

"Did Whitney get accepted?"

Lizbet sniffed and reached for the lace-trimmed linen handkerchief in her robe pocket. "Well, I guess we'll never know."

Bitsy blinked hard and opened her turquoise eyes as wide as they would go. Tilting her head in confusion, she asked Lizbet, "What do you mean, we'll never know?"

Lizbet listlessly picked up an envelope from the corner of the desk and handed it to her friend. "Read my daughter's essay…it's on page 16."

Bitsy sat down on a silk-covered Queen Anne Wing chair and shuffled through the papers Lizbet had given her. She quickly skipped to the middle of the application and then carefully read every word.

Essay Question: There are limitations to what grades, scores and recommendations can tell us about any applicant. We ask you to write a personal essay that will help us to know you better. In the past, candidates have written about their families, intellectual and extracurricular interests, ethnicity or culture, school and community events to which they have had strong reactions, people who have influenced them, significant experiences, personal aspirations, or topics that spring entirely from their imaginations. You should feel confident that in writing about what matters to you, you are bound to convey a strong sense of who you are.

My name is Whitney Wellington Smith, daughter of proud Yale alumni Grant and Lizbet Wellington Smith. It has always been my parents' dream that I follow in their footsteps at your fine institution. But why, you may ask, do I want to apply to Yale? Perhaps the following will give you insight into my thought process.

After months of soul searching, my college decision became crystal clear to me during a recent Memorial Day tradition, the Silent Auction. Many unique items were donated to raise large sums of money for my school. My mother was especially pleased with the many wonderful items she and her committee had solicited that were specifically geared to high school seniors. Parents could choose a basket of dorm necessities for the prospective college Freshman that included a shower caddy, laundry bag, and extra-long twin sheets. Also up for bidding was a brand new cell phone and free nationwide calling plan for one full year. As if that weren't enough, there was a full set of matching luggage for the future college student to use on weekend trips home.

But the biggest draw by far was prominently displayed on a large rectangular table at the far end of the room. Underneath pennants from Harvard, Princeton and Yale were very special bidding sheets. When the Silent Auction officially opened at 8:00 a.m. that Friday before Memorial Day, each of the sheets on that rectangular table immediately filled up. My friend Jonathan's Dad bid a quick $25,000 for guaranteed admission to Princeton. Kate's parents wrote in an even more outrageous amount for Harvard Admission. Taylor's father put his daughter's name and a six-digit sum on the Yale sheet, but he was quickly outbid by my mother.

As the weekend progressed, my parents took shifts and kept vigil on the bidding sheet, quickly topping any amount that appeared. By the time the closing bids were announced that Memorial Day Monday, my parents hugged each other as their names were called to claim the prize of guaranteed acceptance to Yale.

The next thing I was aware of was my mother calling my name over and over and shaking me by the shoulders. "Whitney… Whitney…wake up…why are you screaming?"

Thank God it was just a dream.

So with all due respect, I thank you for taking the time to review my application, but I am withdrawing my (or should I say my parents') request for admission to Yale. With any luck, I hope to be accepted at the college of **my** choice as an incoming Freshman to pursue my own dreams.

Respectfully yours,

Whitney Wellington Smith

Lizbet rose from her chair and walked over to the large picture window. After a long silence spent deep in thought, Lizbet turned to her friend. Bitsy was surprised to see the beginnings of a smile on Lizbet's face.

"Bitsy, I just thought of something. You remember Piper Merriweather? She was that tall, rather plain-looking brunette who pledged the year after we did. She married one of the Kennedy's right after we graduated, remember?" Bitsy nodded, encouraging Lizbet to continue.

The color was returning to the skin covering Lizbet's high cheekbones. "Her family's cabana at Bailey's Beach was right next to the one my parents have had forever. I can't tell you how many summers Piper and I spent together in Newport when we were little girls."

Bitsy wasn't sure why the nostalgic walk down memory lane was making Lizbet feel better, but as long as it was having the desired effect, she most certainly was not going to interrupt. She smiled indulgently.

Pacing back and forth in front of the French doors by the window, Lizbet appeared to be talking to herself. "Doesn't Piper's youngest daughter have an internship in the Admissions Department at Yale while she's getting her graduate degree? If I call Piper and tell her there's been a dreadful mix-up, she can have her daughter just pull Whitney's letter before it reaches the members of the Admissions Committee. I'm sure Piper would be only too happy to do this small favor for me."

Crossing the spacious room, Lizbet sprang into action. "Okay, Bitsy, there's not a moment to lose. Grab that Alumni Phone Directory in the drawer of the desk and get my cell phone from the Louis Vuitton purse hanging on the back of your chair. I'll just run and get dressed so I can look my best when I call Piper."

Pausing in the doorway, Lizbet turned and faced her friend before heading up to the master bedroom suite. "I just can't believe I didn't think of this sooner. It's a scathingly brilliant plan, don't you agree?"

For what was probably the first time in her life, Bitsy was speechless.

~ *The End* ~

0-595-31377-9

Printed in the United Kingdom
by Lightning Source UK Ltd.
101695UKS00001B/216